MW01244443

THE WHOLE BRANZINO

BY

JUD WIDING

APÉRITIF:
WALLY

THE WHOLE BRANZINO

AS **SOON AS** Janis started speaking Latin, Wally Zwillbin went ahead and tuned her out. Languages – unlike people – probably died for a reason, right? Though as Janis was demonstrating, all the academic types were still teaching Latin to each other. Didn't that make it a not-dead language? Apparently not. Wally didn't know. He wasn't an academic type. Oh, he felt himself a fairly intelligent person – smart enough to have avoided a proper job for lo these many years, certainly – but he didn't have any academic accomplishments to his name. Not counting the framed diplomas he'd bought and paid for like racehorses, of courses. He couldn't recite poetry from memory, he couldn't share investment advice, he couldn't weigh in on current events like the Scopes Monkey Trial verdict (he didn't know what the monkey had been charged with, for one). He *certainly* couldn't speak any other languages.

But here was the thing: he was confident. A *confidence man,* one might even say. And as most people rather adorably assumed that there was *any* connection between confidence and intelligence, all Wally ever had to do was claim expertise in something, and hey presto, suddenly he was the expert in the room. Which made him feel quite smart. And didn't it *make* him quite smart, in a way? If he could pull a fast one on those starched shirts who'd wasted years of their lives sniffing books?

He felt so. But there were limits to what could be accomplished, with such a skillset. Duping folks into turning over their life's savings, and/or stealing their watch? Well within Wally's purview.

Exploiting loopholes in the law to free a man who was, it can't be stressed enough, *very obviously guilty* from prison? For that, you needed somebody who could speak a dead language or two.

One of the many reasons Wally so appreciated his lawyer, Janis Kidderminster. She was very much a *loopholes* sort of lawyer. When her time came, and she met St. Peter at those pearly gates, Wally knew two things for certain: that her name would *not* be on the guest list, and that she would have no trouble extemporizing on the inconsistencies in the scriptures, pursuant to introducing a reasonable doubt that heaven had established coherent immigration codes by which her entry could legitimately be barred.

Wally, meanwhile, would just dress up like a delivery

driver and head around to the pearly loading bay, insisting he had three pallets of ham he needed to get to an ice box, pronto, and if they could just point him in the right direction he'd be fine without an escort.

Probably why they made such a good team, she and he. Complimentary skillsets, comparable ethics.

Janis snapped her fingers at Wally. "Pay attention."

He nodded reflexively. "You lost me at the Latin."

"I only said two words in Latin."

"You do have a way of making English *sound* like Latin."

Janis smiled. Wally knew that thin little smirk perfectly well, one his lawyer deployed only to conceal something else entirely. Like a pleasing cheesecloth draped over a chainsaw.

Wally returned her smile. And he actually *meant* his.

"M-*hm.*" Janis leaned back in her chair and tapped her fingertips together. "Well, simplest way I can put it is: I can get this to trial." She sighed at the mere thought of it. "It'll hinge, in no small part, on ambiguity in the phrasing of this particular portion of *Bishop v. Evanston.*" She raised her right pointer finger as she recited the relevant passage, from memory: "And I quote, *'It might have been preferable if the defendant had presen-'*"

"So – and I'm just gonna stop you right there because none of that means anything to me – so you're saying you can honestly get Sammy out of prison?"

"...not *honestly,* no." She picked up some papers from her desk and gave them a half-hearted toss towards the far end of her blotter. "Lucky for us, *honest* and *legal* are barely a Venn diagram."

Wally nodded vacantly.

"…yes," Janis sighed, "I can get Mr. D'Amato out of prison."

"Wow. That's amazing. Only in America, huh? Only in New York!"

"…what?"

"Only in America or New York, I'm saying, can you do various murders and crimes, with fingerprints and witnesses, and they just let you go free."

"…are you interested in hearing the myriad ways you're misrepresenting the *enormous* difficulty I'm going to face, in delivering Mr. D'Amato to his freedom?"

"Not really."

"Okay. Mr. D'Amato is just up the way in Sing Sing at present, correct?"

"…that's right," Wally said, eyeing the tear-away, one-a-day calendar on Janis' desk. Whereas some such models Wally had seen featured a new joke every day, or a new uplifting aphorism, Janis' calendar seemed to present only the names of legal cases. No information on the substance or the verdict, just the name. Today's was *Plifton v. The United States Department of Agriculture*. "For a few more hours, anyway." He returned his gaze to Janis. "They're transferring him to Vermont tomorrow."

"Vermont?" Janis groaned. "I was assured he would only be rotated through states in which he had been con-victed of a crime!"

"I think that's just how it is."

"…what the hell did he do in Vermont?"

"There's not much to do up there, so probably all of it." Wally narrowed his eyes. "Shouldn't you know that?"

Janis grimaced at him, then looked towards her office window and tapped her fingers some more.

It occurred to Wally that maybe having worn a funny square hat and shaken the hand of a university president didn't preclude one from leading with confidence. And come to think of it…he didn't actually know where Janis was meant to have gone to law school. She had paperwork framed on the walls of her office, but Wally had never looked at any of it too carefully…

"Hey," Janis snapped, without her fingers this time.
Wally turned to her.

Janis turned back to the window. "The trial certainly won't be any time soon, but I had Eric run everything over to the courthouse this afternoon. First thing tomorrow, they'll at least be required to transfer Mr. D'Amato out of Sing Sing, to somewhere a bit more comfortable. Keeping him in New York State, as well."

"I don't imagine comfort is much of an issue for him. But he'll appreciate being close to home, I know."

"Mhm. Would you mind putting the paperweight back on my desk?"

"What?"

Janis turned to Wally. Pointed through the desk, at his lap. "It's not real gold."

"What's that?" Wally made a show of patting his pants pockets, and, to his *astonishment,* finding a seemingly-but-apparently-not-actually gold paperweight, a half-sphere with a mahogany base that also probably wasn't real. And he was, to be fair, genuinely astonished. "Sorry," he said, returning the paperweight to the table. "Sometimes the hands have a mind of their own. You know how it is."

"I don't."

"A golden paperweight's weird, huh?"

"It's not gold, I told you."

Wally shrugged, poked the paperweight a few times, then flinched and checked his watch, a gen-u-ine Rolex Oyster that he'd used as the model for the coun-ter-feit ones he had in a briefcase in his car. "I think I can get to Sing Sing before visiting hours are up."

"Why would you go to Sing Sing?" Janis wondered, in a tone most often deployed with the word *don't*.

"Just to give Sammy the good news."

Janis shook her head. "No point. You can't arrange a prison visit on the day of."

"Oh, I know. I figured I'd bribe a guard to get him the message."

"All that'd do is risk word getting out of what we're doing."

"Yeah, but I don't see how that matters here. We're not doing anything illegal. I mean, by definition, isn't anything a lawyer does *legal?*"

The way Janis spun around in her chair was most definitely an answer.

Wally blinked. "I'm just worried, having known him for long enough, I'm worried if we don't give him the high sign to sit tight, he might *do something*. That'd, you know...not quite honor... all of your paperwork."

Rolling her head slowly, Janis fixed Wally with an

expression of vague amusement.

"As far as he knows," Wally continued, "I'm just saying, he thinks he's still working on a hundred life sentences. Since he doesn't know about your paperwork. And I'm just saying, knowing the guy like I do…he's got one more night close to home, and he's got nothing to lose. As far as he knows."

"What are you worried he'll do? *Break out* of one of the *highest-security prisons* on the *planet?*"

"Yep."

"…"

"It'd just be pretty frustrating if he did it the day before you were gonna get him out legally, right? Or start to, at any rate. Just because he hadn't heard word one about your paperwork."

"The odds of him breaking out of *Sing Sing* are infinitesimally small as-is. That he would happen to do it *tonight*, even more so."

"He's got a real knack for bad timing, is all I'm saying. Knowing the guy."

"I know the guy too."

"…I mean, you *do,* but not in the same way."

Janis frowned.

"I'm not saying you don't know him, I'm just saying, you know. The history you and Sammy have is like…the history of the telephone. In terms of recency. Whereas what he and I have is more like the history of just cupping your hands around your mouth and yelling across a big river." He paused. "It's a *lot* like that, actually."

Janis wrestled a smirk off of her face. "He'll be fine,"

she insisted. "It'll be a nice surprise for him. Early birthday present, here, we got you a trial. And shortly thereafter, freedom." Her expression slackened slightly. "Precisely when *is* his birthday?"

Wally scratched his forehead. "He usually likes to have it in the winter."

Right on cue: a songbird fluttered down onto the windowsill and whistled a paean to the crispness of a Spring afternoon. At least, might have done, if the window had been open.

The *thunk* of its crashing into the glass had a musical quality to it, at least.

Wally smiled at Janis' ear. "Well, that is the best way to surprise a fella with his birthday gift, I suppose, is give it to him on the wrong end of the calendar."

Janis just frowned at the splotch left on the window the bird's botched entry. Eyes locked on that splotch, she said "put the paperweight *back,* Mr. Zwillbin."

"Sorry. Nervous habit now."

Janis rolled her eyes back to Wally and sighed. "All he has to do is be *in prison* for one more night than he has been already. The risk of giving him the high-sign is greater than the potential reward." She chuckled to herself. "I ask again: what are the odds he'd plan an escape for the *very night* before we've finally got him on the path to legal freedom? This *same* night?"

Wally scratched at the spot just above his right ear. Boy, Janis really *didn't* know Sammy very well.

STEP ONE:
PRE-HEAT

THE WHOLE BRANZINO

1

SING SING'S about as tough as its fuckin name. Where's the law says you got a maximum security joint, you gotta give it a fuckin goofball name? Sing Sing. Yellow Onion. Sloop Huff. Maybe they're figurin the dumb name's gonna make a tough think twice about springin himself. Ain't nobody wants to say they broke outta a joint called some shit like Zucchini Heehaw, on accounta that's the same as coppin to you had a stretch where Zucchini Heehaw had ya beat.

Ain't the name kept me from flyin the coop til tonight though. First off, I ain't gonna make any breaks mean I gotta break any guards. Parta my fuckin predicament here is I accidentally squashed a cop, though in my defense, who the fuck's takin a load off under a car when a bruiser's halfway to flippin it? That ain't on me. More ways than one, it's on him. Get it? Rest his soul, he seemed like a nice enough guy, for a fuckin cop.

I ain't gonna lie, that one kept me up nights. Ain't much out there's gonna keep me from sleepin when I got a mind to, but killin folks I ain't meant to kill? That ain't the sorta thing's fuckin conducive to the wooly white headcount, you see what I'm sayin. Sheep. You get it.

So anyways, what I'm sayin is, I ain't lookin to brain any fuckin guards on my way to the see-ya-later. Some fellas in here figure me for some kinda soft on that score. I always ask em do they wanna help a pal out and reconsider their figure, on accounta I get fuckin bored in solitary.

Oh, speak of the fuckin red guy, it's only Skip on his left-to-right. Just prior to lights-out, the guards all take a constitutional, make sure are all us crooks in our cages or what. Here in C Ward, up on floor three, Skip's the dick what promenades past my fuckin cell. Only ever walks past goin the one way. Left to right. Ain't like I'm scratchin my head how, there's stairs at both ends of the fuckin walkway up here. Just a funny fuckin detail.

I says to him Evenin Skip, on accounta he's a human bein and not a fuckin terrier mix like you mighta figured from the name.

Skip says to me Evening D'Amato.

That's all's he ever fuckin said to me, til the mornin when we do it again, only we're sayin Mornin to each other. We're just tellin each other what time of day is it, and what's each other's name. Still, Skip's alright. He's just a fella doin a job, answerin to a dog's name. So you see how come I ain't lookin to bust outta here in a way means I gotta rip Skip in half to do it.

That's the first thing's got me waitin til tonight for my break. Had to figure out how am I gonna do it without I gotta rip Skip in half. Second thing though, is they're puntin me elsewheres tomorrow. One of them little states up on the hey-how-are-ya arm of this great fuckin nation. That ain't a vacation I fuckin recall takin, but hey, they got the fingertip prints prove I paid a visit, so the fuck do I know.

The fuck I know is I got no clue when am I gonna be this close to the city again. New York, I oughta say, in case you figured I was talkin about fuckin Danbury or some shit. I got a pal in the city there...well, I got a bunch of fuckin pals there, but the pal I'm thinkin of is a fella called Raheeq. He hails from whatever they're callin the old sandy bits of Asia used to be Ottoman but ain't no more on accounta they didn't do so good in the war. I one time asked him did he ever meet that Lawrence fella. Raheeq looks at me like I'm fuckin dim, so I says to him *Lawrence* louder than the first time. He asks me T.E.? I says I'll take coffee if you got it. Raheeq said to me No, *T.E.* louder than the first time. I says The fuck are you laughin at? Daff and Wally were there too, *they* had a big old laugh at that. I let em only on accounta those are two of my best pals. Well, Daff's the lady what do I conjugate with. Sets her some ways off from the other pals. I don't conjugate with the other pals. Specially not Wally. Not that I'm, you know, I'm not sayin specially not him like there's somethin *wrong* with him. Just, he and me got a friendship goes back a ways. Be a shame to screw it up conjugatin.

Anyways, Raheeq, I'm sayin about Raheeq and his restaurant what's called Rahino's on accounta it ain't exactly in a neighborhood's gonna take kindly to the squiggly writin, I'm sayin about him on accounta the second thing's scheduled my Sing Sing Swan Song for tonight is I got a fuckin hankerin. Like ladies say when they're in a family way, they get a hankerin for some food. That ain't the word what do they use, only I can't fuckin recall what's the word I want so I'm goin with hankerin and you gotta come with. There's a word means you just want some kinda foodstuff real bad, and all of a sudden I'm figurin on takin my leave and CRAVIN, holy shit, that's the word. I got a cravin, for the whole branzino at Raheeq's.

You ever had branzino? It's a fuckin fish. Well, I got no clue is the branzino the fish or is it the way how do they cook the fish, but either way you say Lemme get a branzino and they bring you a fuckin fish tastes like, ooh, I ain't got the words. Only thing is, ain't everywhere's gonna bring ya branzino like everywhere else. You been to Davio & Sons uptown? Might be outta your price range, seein how you dress, but lemme tell ya, they play with your food before they give it to ya. Cut out the bones, twist off the head, lay it on a bed of fuckin chives or some shit. You wanna fondle my food prior to it's in the oven or wherever the fuck ya put it, that's the chef's call. But the fuck are you doin stickin your filthy little fingers in my dinner right prior to ya bring it to me? The fuck is that?

Raheeq's gonna give ya the whole branzino. You says

to him Lemme get the branzino, he brings you the fuckin branzino. Bones, head, tail. First time I got it, Raheeq tells me Eat the eyes. I says to him Fuck you, *you* eat the eyes. And he does. Now I eat the eyes, on accounta I ain't payin for I'm just gonna watch this guy eat little delicacies.

Anyway, forget the eyes. I'm a whole branzino guy. Scoopin out the bones and twistin off the head's as bad as chewin my steak for me. I can take out the fuckin bones myself. Don't believe me, I got corroboration. Most of it's about four feet under the Barrens.

So whatever, the then-to-here is every night I'm stayin awake in all these goofy-name places they got me in, and I'm thinkin to myself how'm I gonna get out in a way ain't gonna mean splittin Skip. Metaphorically, I ain't met Skip til Sing Sing. But then I get to Sing Sing, where can I hear the Hudson babblin past, and it says to me Just thirty miles to Manhattan, and now I'm thinkin Man, I'd kill for a whole branzino at Rahino's. And if I ain't bein literal, I'm comin right the fuck up to it. So that got me thinkin different than I did at the other joints. And now I'm puttin a plan together. Slow and smart. Ain't nobody gotta get so much as bonked. And I got a branzino waitin for me at the end, with the bones and delicacies and all that.

So we're at tonight now. I been settin up this plan for six fuckin months. Feelin good about it. Am I sweatin about is it gonna go well? No. It's too fuckin airtight a plan for me to be sweatin about is it gonna go well. I'm ready for it.

It's gonna work. Tonight's the fuckin night.
I'm doin the plan.

2

LOTTA THINGS YOU GOTTA GET prior to you're
gonna bust outta Sing Sing without killin nobody. Yeah, I'm gonna tell you about the fuckin
breakout, relax about that. I just wanna say the whole
thing at ya, far as the setup goes. So you get it all and
you're sayin to yourself, Wow, this Samuzzo guy's pretty
fuckin smart.

First thing I did was I got a lot of haircuts. You want
a haircut, who do you figure's gonna give it to ya? I'll tell
ya, they let the jailbirds do it. No shit, they take two fellas
in their fuckin maximum security hoosegow, give one of
em a pair of snippers, point em at the other one, and wish
em both good luck. And hey, ain't nobody ever sliced off
anybody else's ears. Maybe prison *does* work. Anyway
though, what I'm gettin at is there ain't no guards in the
snipshop when I get my trim, so I ain't gotta be too
fuckin inconspicuous about I'm pickin up my clippins
off the floor.

Guy who gives me the trim's called Tear, which I
gotta figure ain't his real name, just one he figured sounded tough, and furthermore I gotta figure he ain't got the
literacies on accounta if you read his name, now you
gotta wonder is this a guy who rips stuff or does he just
cry a lot. Anyway, Tear, as in the rippin kind, he sees me

scoopin my own hair off the floor and he asks me Samuzzo, what are you doing?

So I says to him Woah, how'd you recognize me?

He asks me Huh?

I says On accounta you made me look like a new man.

Now I fuckin flattered him, on accounta there's the second thing you gotta get for the bust-out, after you got your own clippins: a prison pal.

Third thing is time. You gotta plan this stuff way out front. Set the fuckin stage. Otherwise you ain't gonna be half ready like you oughta when it turns out tonight's the night. My thing is, ya gotta make it a fuckin practice. I done this every place I been, not just Sing Sing. Gettin the feel for it. That way you wake up one day and you look in the no-glass-havin mirror and the mirror says to ya Tonight's the fuckin night, you can say to the mirror No thanks to you, ya louse, I done all the fuckin work.

Fourth thing is arts and fuckin crafts. On accounta they let us do some arts and fuckin crafts in prison, how you like that? You better like it, on accounta all these fuckin pencils and construction papers? That's your tax money, tough guy. See how come I don't bother with that shit?

Anyway, you wanna break out, you gotta get good at the arts and crafts. That way, the guards look over, they see you slappin clay on a table or pushin charcoal around a piece of paper, all what can they say to themselves is Samuzzo's up to his old tricks. I gotta figure once I'm out maybe the warden ain't gonna be so generous about sharin his fuckin crayons with the guys what're still in here, but all the same it ain't my fault those fellas ain't never figured out how're they gonna use their arts and crafts to bust out.

So anyway, then it's the night, and I'm gonna tell ya how'd the breakout go now. See? Like I said I would.

Skip and I do our Evenin routine, then somebody down on the first floor shouts at us Lights Out. Seems kinda fuckin wasteful far as breath goes, on accounta the Lights go Out same time every night, and even if you can't figure time half-well, you always know when's it Lights Out on accounta the Lights go Out.

Hour into Lights Out, I'm worried maybe the second thing ain't gonna be first like it's gotta be. Second thing's the prison pal, like I fuckin said. Tear. He's one cell block over. Caught him in the yard some weeks back and I said to him When I tell ya tonight's the night, you make a fuckin seizure or some shit round nine, I'll check in on anybody you got needs checkin in on. He said to me his wife and kids. I said to him sure. Then I told him when's the night gonna be, on accounta I already knew when was it. Then I told him again today, Don't fuckin forget, tonight's the night.

Only I'm figurin it could be he still fuckin forgot. On accounta I got a quality clock in my head, and it's tickin right the fuck through nine. Two guards in my block still. I can hear em talkin. Ain't nobody gone runnin one block over. Only I know there ain't no way the two guards in Tear's block are gonna handle a real big guy herkin and jerkin so hard he's crackin the concrete underneath. I figured, gonna take at least one guy leavin my block for sure. So…fuck. I was really countin on Tear for

I hear one of the guards go runnin. His little footsteps goin clop clop clop. Then, fuckin right, they're *both* runnin.

I roll off my cot and I swear I got my hand underneath the frame prior to the ground can tell my knees ouch. I pull out my fuckin masterpiece – and I gotta toot my own fuckin horn on this. Every day I'm doin my arts and crafts like I mentioned, I been pretendin to be a little loopy so when I slap a piece of fuckin plaster on my face and let it get crunchy, nobody says boo. Stuff that in my pocket, take it back to my cell. I rip a little hole in my mattress, just a teeny fuckin slot, and stick the plaster in. You can't feel nothin funny to lay on the thing, and even if some brainiac figures to cut it open and scopes the crunchy chunks, they don't look like shit. Even when I'm addin another piece, then another and another, all I gotta do is say Where the fuck you buyin your mattresses from? and there ain't nothin they can ding me on.

Nobody got any kind of wise though. So today I put the pieces together with some glue I ain't lookin to mention how'd I get it in here cept to say there wasn't no room for error, on accounta there wasn't hardly room for the fuckin tube.

Anyways, you glue the plaster slaps together, and it don't look like nothin at all. But in the Lights Out, on its side, with all them hair clippins what'd I pocket from the trimatorium stuck on top and some pillows under the blanket where there oughta be a body…

I gotta say, for a mess of arts supplies? You ask me,

looks like Samuzzo's still in bed. And you ask me twice, I'll tell ya this cell ain't big enough for two Samuzzi. Ain't nowhere big enough for two Samuzzi. I ain't about to draw a line similarizes me and a tube of glue in a tight squeeze, but this cell ain't hardly big enough for the *one* Samuzzo.

But you know, how am I gonna get outta the cell? It ain't like I'm gonna just turn sidewise and cartwheel between the bars. Furtherfuckinmore, it ain't like I can just rip em outta the wall on accounta the noise'd be

Yeah, obviously I already know how'm I gonna get out, I'm just settin it up. For *you.* Dramatic-wise. How the fuck's he gonna get outta this one, ya know. All these fuckin obstacles.

Ok, I'm settin it up on accounta the thing I done ain't so splashy: I been scratchin away the bars on the windows. I done fuckin math and figured, lemme just get all four bars out, that's a hole I can squeeze through. So I got me a fuckin nail file, which we ain't supposta have in here but it ain't like Sing Sing's fulla fellas read the rules cover to cover. So I get the file through means I ain't keen to mention and I start doin just one fuckin scratch at a time. One night, I know this ain't too bright only I figured it was kinda funny, one night I done it while Skip was doin his rounds. I scratched so's the scratch happened whenever he took a step. He stopped walkin, I stopped scratchin. He walked faster, I scratched faster. Yeah I mighta got caught, but I didn't. I did fuckin laugh though. You gotta get your giggles in Sing Sing anywhere ya can.

Anyway, like I was sayin, this is a good for instance on how come you gotta plan ahead so far. I did just a few scratches on the bars in the window every night. Add up enough nights, and the bars're rattlin like baby teeth doin a sultry yoo-hoo at the fairy.

I yank the bars outta the window. It's so fuckin easy. I don't know how come people ain't doin this more often. I lay em real gentle under my cot, only I just about scream Aaaaah out loud when I turn around on accounta I forgot I was gonna see myself layin in bed there, bein made outta plaster paper. Then I turn back and frown at the open window. How's it look fuckin smaller without the bars? I done the math, I know I'm gonna fit…but it ain't gonna be comfy. Fuckin thing's what, two feet across? I don't figure it was much more.

I stick my head through and look down. Remember how I said to ya I'm on the third floor? Well, that ain't changed since I mentioned it. I can't just climb through the window and jump, or I'm hittin the dirt at a speed puts my hips through my shoulders. Fences they got just over yonder ain't gonna slow me down none, unless I got my hips through my shoulders.

Only that ain't a fuckin problem on accounta I been plannin ahead, like I keep tellin ya. Workin on grip strength. See, they got the windows stacked one on top of the other, all the way to the ground. Got my window, then maybe, what, nine feet under that they got another. Then another. Then you're hittin the dirt. So I figure, I climb out my window, then I drop down, grab the bars of the window under mine, drop again, grab, drop, dirt.

Maybe that ain't the smartest fuckin way down, on accounta it's so dark I can't see shit, and if I ain't grabbin right when I gotta then I'm cooked, but what's my fuckin otherwise? You got any fuckin idea how much I weigh? I ain't tyin bedsheets together and doin a fuckin Rapunzel. Though I do got my hair on the assist, so I guess the lady and I do got somethin in common.

I'm stallin. On accounta I'm nervous. Not about the plan overall. Just the heights bit here. I ain't too tough to say so, I ain't good with heights. Plus…hell, how'm I gonna turn around for the grippage?

I look down again. Even though it's Lights Out for the sky right now, I can still see the dirt. Three floors down. Ah, fuck.

I reach through the window and smile on accounta the night's nice and cool for my mitts. Sing Sing ain't got the best ventilation you ever felt, so you get feelin that fresh air again? Sweet like fuckin crumb cake.

That's enough of that though. I turn my hands so's my thumbs are pointin down and my palms are facin out, then grab tight to the outside edges of the window. Wrap my fingertips around the fresh air side of the brick. Start pullin.

So we got a fuckin obstacle straight off. When I done the math, I didn't figure how'm I gonna make my body fit the numbers. Mostly on accounta my math's less numbers than it is shapes. Window's a rectangle, I'm a rectangle. Perfect fuckin fit.

Drillin down though, I see the way I'm figurin to pull my body-rectangle through the window-rectangle is, I gotta bunch my elbows into my sides. That ain't gonna work. Only if I try wrigglin straight through with my arms in fronta me, how'm I gonna do a mid-air do-si-do quick enough so's I can grab the ledge?

Feet first. Course. I go through feet first, hands last.

Takes some doin, but I finally figure I gotta put my hands on the ground like it's drop and give me twenty, then plant my feet on the wall and fuckin reverse-walk em up towards the window. So I do that. I get my feet through the window then, and I look like I'm ready for a fuckin wheelbarrow race, pointin fuckin diagonal with my shoes out the window and my hands on the floor.

Now...fuck. Ain't nothin to it but to do it.

I do the hardest fuckin pushup you ever heard about, launchin my torso up and back at the window.

For a second I'm worried did I push so hard I'm gonna launch myself straight out the fuckin hole in the wall, only my shoulders're wide enough they stick against the sides. I collect my fuckin self, then shimmy out, tryin not to kick my feet against the outside wall too much while I'm lowerin em out the window.

Shimmy shimmy shimmy and I'm hangin from my window by my meathooks. Okay. Ain't no goin back now. Well, that ain't true – I still got return tickets til I drop to the next window. Which, fuck me, I figured it was gonna be dark, but I ain't figured it was gonna be the kinda dark's so dark it makes your ears ring. Where's the fuckin moon when you need it?

So I'm droppin blind. Fine by me. Feel's what matters anyway.

JUD WIDING

I take a loud nosebreath in. Tell my teeth to quit grindin, less they wanna give the whole fuckin game up. Then I start gettin dizzy. Like I'm gonna fuckin pass out. Wha...oh. I let the nosebreath out.

Then I drop.

Jesus, the wind's louder than how'd I fuckin remember it. I let go and all of a sudden I'm

Fuck I feel the ledge of the first window I gotta grab slip straight past my fuckin fingers. Bonks em hard, all but fuckin rips off the nail of my right middle.

This ain't good. I just fell a whole fuckin story without

I can't stop myself sayin GAH when I grab the bars of the next window down, the one's on the first story cell. I wasn't plannin on hittin a window quite so fast like I did. If my arms ain't both outta their fuckin sockets, they can't be more'n few gristlebits shy. Jesus the fuck Lapedus, that shit *hurts*.

I quit groanin and peek in at the fella in the cell. He's fast asleep. Ain't heard nothin out here. I turn so my ear's pointin through the window. I don't hear nothin in there.

All good.

My teeth are askin me can they get back to grindin and I let em, on accounta that way I'm only groanin when I lower myself onto the ground, instead of shoutin.

Then my feet touch the dirt, and it's laughin I gotta be worried about.

I knock my shoulders against the outside wall of fuckin Sing Sing, *hard,* so's they'll pop back into their sockets. Only I don't figure they was out at all. Turns out I just made my fuckin shoulders hurt worse, knockin em against the wall for no fuckin reason. Really wish I ain't done the second one especially.

So the fences do slow me down a little, I oughta mention, on accounta my fuckin shoulders, plus I ain't remembered about the barbed wires they got on top. I get over alright, but I ain't laughin no more.

3

HONESTY'S THE BEST FUCKIN POLICY. Might not seem like I'm the sorta schmuck says stuff like that, but I am. I don't fuckin lie, cept when I have to.

So I'm freshly flown in my striped pajamas, walkin down the road headin towards Manhattan, when behind me I got the headlamps of a jalopy tryin to break up the woods. I figure it ain't gonna serve me a fuckin whit, takin a header into the sticks. So I just wait for the hoopdyscoot wheezes up to me and I flag down the old-timer behind the wheel.

He cranks down his window and he asks me What the hell are you doing out here, son? In your undergarments, no less?

I says to him I just busted outta Sing Sing, I'm tryin to get me a whole branzino.

The old-timer laughs and says In the city?

I says to him You know anywhere's servin branzino in these fuckin boonies?

He laughs again and he says Seriously, you know

you're near the prison, right? It's dangerous out here.

I says to him Only since I busted out.

This guy can't fuckin contain himself. He giggles and says to me Alright, be that way. Let's get you to your dinner.

See what I'm sayin, far as honesty goes?

4

OLD-TIMER'S NAME turns out to be James. James is a fuckin stand-up fella, he drives me all the way to Manhattan, even right up to Rahino's, and wishes me a fond fuckin farewell. I tell him the same and we don't never cross paths again, so you can forget about James.

Raheeq shutters around ten. Early for an eatery in the city, huh? His place his rules, but still, the fuck? Anyways, it's a ways after ten, so I bang on the door. I yell Raheeq! in case he thought I got the wrong address.

I gotta bang for a good thirty seconds prior to somebody opens the door. It ain't Raheeq. Just some little kid I figure for Raheeq's little nephew, even if he ain't in point of fuckin fact a little nephew.

The kid looks me up and down and up again and says We're closed? Like he ain't sure.

So I says to him You go tell Uncle Raheeq Samuzzo's here.

Then the door swings all the way open and Raheeq's been standin behind it the whole fuckin time.

I says to him Some fuckin sense of hospitality you got.

He gives me the once over and says What are you doing here?

I smile on accounta I forgot how much I appreciate Raheeq's speechism. The fuckin accent. He always kinda sounds like he's talkin down to ya, on accounta even when he's askin a question he ends on a lower note than what'd he start on.

I says to him I was in the fuckin neighborhood and I figured

He interrupts me and he says You were in jail, yes?

So I says No, I just heard wearin stripes flatters my fuckin figure.

Raheeq looks over my fuckin figure, this way'n that, then he says somethin in a language don't mean nothin to me, then in English he says to me Oh no, come inside, come inside.

So I do.

Then he asks me So…you were in the prison, and then you are free, and first thing you say is, before I do anything, I must visit a restaurant?

I says to him Yuh, cept instead of just any old restaurant I was comin to visit yours.

He asks me Did you…

So I fill in for him You wanna know did I kill somebody for my get-out?

He nods.

I says to him Course not. Then I explain to him the whole bust-out, with the plaster me on the cot with the hair and everythin, and the whole thing with droppin out

33

the window.

Raheeq listens real careful as he's walkin me over to a table in his dim little fuckin dinin area. Then he says But why did you make yourself in the bed?

I says So in case they look in prior to they take prison attendance tomorrow, it looks like I'm sleepin.

He says to me But if they look into your cell, they will not see the window has been removed?

I take a few seconds to think about that. And by a few I mean thirty. Then after thirty seconds is done I says to Raheeq That's a point you got there. I ain't thought of that.

Raheeq just nods.

I says to him So how bout that whole branzino there, pal?

Raheeq sighs like he means it and he says How will you pay, hm? I do not accept cigarettes.

I says to him Real funny, cigarettes. Then I ask him You got a phone?

He says Of course I have a phone.

I says to him Great, gimme two whole branzinos and show me where's the phone.

He does, so I ring up one of the fake numbers Wally's got. I mean, the number ain't fake, but the name on it is.

Nobody answers. That's alright, I didn't figure I'd get it in one. He's got so many fuckin hideouts and safehouses. And I got the numbers for *all* of em in my fuckin memory. I'm just hopin he ain't added too many new ones since I been inside.

I ring-a-ding the next one. Then the next. Then the

next. Then you get the idea.

Eventually I call one that says ring ring and then click and then McBintiff's All-Hours Accountancy, in Wally's voice. Groggy, like I woke him up.

I says to the phone Guess who?!

The phone says …

So I says Wouldya believe me if I said they let me out for the good behaviors?

Wally says to me Oh no, Sammy. Real sharp, like he's wide awake now.

I says to him You're right, they ain't done that. Say, you wanna swing by Raheeq's joint with some cash? We got two whole branzinos on the

He interrupts me and says Oh *no*, Sammy.

I says You don't want bones in yours or somethin? Since when the fuck don't you like a whole branzino?

I hear Wally's makin a bunch of sputterin sounds, so I says to him Less you already got some fish bones you're fuckin chokin on.

He says to me Good to hear from ya, buddy, but, uh, I think you just made the biggest mistake of your entire life.

I says to him How's that?

He says You broke out?

I says to him Yeah I fuckin broke out, you wanna tell me how come're you makin like that's the biggest boner in history, me breakin out?

Get this, he says to me We were gonna get you out tomorrow. Start the process to, anyway.

I says Well I got myself out tonight, and we got two

whole branzinos on the cooktop, so how about you get on down

He interrupts me and he says We don't have time for branzinos, Sammy. He says it real serious. And on top of that, it ain't often does he ever interrupt me.

I don't say nothin to that, til I say What'd I do, Wally?

He says I need you to come to my apartment, right now.

I ask him which one does he mean.

He tells me which one does he mean. Then he says stuff like Oh *man* and Oh *no* a bunch of times.

I put my hand on the talky part of the phone and I ask Raheeq How long we got on the whole branzinos there?

Raheeq calls to me One hour, more, less?

So I take my hand off the talky part and I says to Wally Alright, I can get there in somethin like an hour. Either more or less.

And he says to me This time of night, it's a ten minute cab ride.

I says to him How fast is this fuckin cab goin?

He says You're calling from Rahino's right? That's ten minutes at a normal speed.

I let him know If you give me an hour, I can bring two whole branzinos with

He interrupts me *again* and real solemnwise he says I'll meet you at my apartment. I'll try to get there lickity-split, but I might be closer to a jiffy. I won't take a full hour, though. Let yourself in when you get there, and just... don't panic.

I says to him I ain't panickin. I don't know what am I supposed to panic about. I'm a free fuckin man, either way.

He says You're not, though. You're a fugitive now. The cops will be dogging you for the rest of your life. But Janis was about to get you out free and clear, back to a *normal* life. Oh, *man*. This is bad, Sammy. This is not desirable.

I ask him So how's it gonna help I go to your apartment?

He says We'll figure something out. We always do. Remember that time you accidentally boarded a trans-atlantic steamer to Morocco, and I impersonated the Secretary of State so you wouldn't have to pay for a return ticket?

I says No. What? When was that?

He says It was right after you got back from the war. You thought you were getting on the Staten Island Ferry, but that was not the case.

I says Oh, yeah. And they wanted to make like I was a fuckin molerat for some other country, right?

He says Nope, that was the time you thought you were getting on the Staten Island Ferry, but you accidentally got on a Navy submarine going to perform test dives off Long Island Sound.

I says Oh.

He says to me Those were both real jams, but we got you out of them.

I says I guess you're right about that.

He says This is much worse than those were, though.

I says Oh again.

We talk for a bit longer, Wally convincin me of the wisdom of I oughta leave the fuckin fish and get me to his apartment. Time comes when I say See ya, and I put the phone back in its fuckin cradle. Then I walk into the kitchen and tell Raheeq I figure I gotta take a rain check on those fuckin whole branzinos.

Raheeq don't sound too happy, only I ain't really listenin. I'm just lookin at the two fishies layin on the counter. They're both lookin at me with their fuckin delicacies. I wanna tell him to close their eyes, only they ain't got lids, do they? Do fish blink?

I ask Raheeq Do fish blink?

He blinks at me, only he don't answer.

Then I point to the fish I says to em I'll be back for you, you delicious fishy fucks.

Then I look back to Raheeq and I ask him Any chance I can bum some fuckin cab fare off ya?

He keeps on doin what was he doin just a second ago.

5

I BORROWED A FUCKIN SHAWL from Raheeq to cover up my striped pajamas, only it don't even occur to me til I'm halfway to Wally's new pad that somebody might recognize my fuckin mug. I never figured it for halfway memorable most of my life – woulda said my below-the-neck's what do folks notice first-through-fifth about me. I'm a big guy, can't recall did I mention that. But I'll tell ya, you cheese off the paid-by-taxes types what know a greyscale doodler and some folks at the papers? Fuck me, next thing you know they got a real serious scribble of your face in the funny pages, and *everybody's* got flawless fuckin recall as to how far apart're your peepers.

I don't figure my face's been like the joke since the feds got my whole fuckin corpus doin a tour of their best lockups, but people got long memories, seems like.

You know that joke? Black and white and red all over? Only its like book-read on accounta they sound the same? And the setup's what do you call a penguin just got his throat slashed or somethin? And only also its gotta do with the paper? Joke goes somethin like that. The fuck do I know, I ain't a guy tells jokes. You figure it out.

What I'm gettin at is, the guy drivin the cab says to me You look familiar.

I says to him Is that right?

He says Yeah. I can see his eyes in the little mirror lookin up and down, up and down. He says You in the pictures?

So I says Not if I can help it.

I can't figure what the fuck's he chucklin at. Either he don't get my meanin, or he *does*, and on that second of the two I don't figure he'd be chucklin.

Only ain't been too long since I learned the hard way, there ain't no percentage in bein a hard-ass if you ain't gotta. So I just make a little chucklin noise too, even though I ain't in the same fuckin phylum as The Chucklin Type. I turn and chuckle at the window, which turns out has my fuckin reflection on it. My fuckin face. Hell, I really shoulda figured on the whole bein recognized thing. That's a hell of a fuckin whaddyacallthat. An oversight. Only *over's* gonna mean *too much* mostly, right? My problem ain't too much sight. It's too little. I made a fuckin undersight, is what I done.

The driver says Ooh! I know who you are.

I can tell from his voice he *definitely* don't, so I do another chuckle and I ask him Who's that then?

He says Bigelow Cooper.

I says to him The guy from the pictures? After I just fuckin said to you I ain't in the pictures?

He nods at his little mirror.

I ask him That fat motherfucker? This is *muscle*. I look like a fat motherfucker to you?

Driver just shrugs and says somethin about how the mirror distorts the proportionalities.

I wanna tell him somethin about how I'll distort *his* proportionalities, only that ain't fuckin doin, on accounta this is what was Wally warnin me about. Bein a lam guy for my whole life. A guy on the lam. Gotta tread light when you're a lam guy. Not sayin nothin crosswise to nobody, so they don't look at ya longer than they're gonna.

Ah, hell, I ain't a guy can live on the run. On accounta I'm a guy what can other guys spot from paces off. Sure, I'm outta the big house, but if I'm spendin my life bein a fuckin lam guy…how far am I gonna get? Or maybe it oughta be, how far do I gotta *go?* Sure as hell can't stay in the tristate, on accounta I plan on steppin outside sometimes, and folks're liable to finger me by just my fuckin shadow. Only I like the tri-state. *Daff,* my girl who'd I already tell you about, likes the tri-state. She's got her own damn life here. She really gonna go with me, become a fuckin lam gal? On accounta I ain't lookin to be a lam guy without she comes with, on the lam. And the fuck's the *lam,* anyway?

Shit. I really fuckin stepped in it this time, I figure.

Feelin the need for I gotta be discreet, I says to the guy up front You got me. Bang to rights. I'm Bigelow fuckin Cooper, from the pictures.

The driver says to me Nice to meet you. What was it like working with Bebe Daniels?

I sigh real loud and says A dream.

6

WALLY'S NEW PAD'S on the third floor. He said that to me on the phone, I just forgot to tell you about he said that to me. Ain't like it matters, I'm just scenin the set for ya.

Anyway, I'm walkin up the stairs and I almost trip over this fuckin cat's decided sixth step from the top's as good a place as any to take a fuckin load off. I feel it under my shoe in time for I can lift my foot up, only I gotta flop onto all fours to keep from squashin the fuckin thing. Now I'm on hands and fuckin knees with the cat usin me for a fuckin parasol. Just sittin under my fuckin gut, lookin up at me like You ain't from around here huh?

So I says to the cat Ain't nobody ever told you stairs're a means? Opposite to a fuckin end?

The cat says to me Meer, all high-pitched like. Some kinda fuckin cute, lemme tell ya.

I get back on my two feet and I says to the cat Just get off the fuckin stairs already, Jesus. Then I step over it and hike the resta the way to Wally's door. He was sayin to me he's sure I can figure out how do I get in – well that's fuckin moot on account the door's unlocked. Gonna have to have a word with the guy about that. This ain't a parta town you wanna let any fuckin grapefruit turn your doorknob without he's gotta fight for it. And when I'm talkin about this parta town, I'm talkin about the whole of the fuckin tri-state what do I love so much.

So I turn the doorknob and open the door and there's a gun in my fuckin face.

I reach out and grab for it, only the gun zooms back outta my fuckin reach as I'm reachin. It's a big long sorta boomer's got a wide mouth and a sensitive fuckin trigger. I seen the type before. Normal-wise, I'm all sortsa giddy bout guns in my face. Take em, break em, then all you got left is the sorta person's got no clue how do they fight if they ain't got firepower.

Only I ain't so giddy now, on accounta I ain't never had a gun in my face gettin pulled back by the person's got the gun to begin with.

Fuck, my fat ass ain't slowin down now, is it? In addition to bein fuckin fat, like the guy from the pictures?

The person's got the gun is a lady looks like the type of lady what's a fella with a top hat and a long handkerchief gonna put in a box and cut down the middle with a comedy saw. Gun's just about her-sized, and I can tell from the way she's got it racked into her shoulder, she knows how to use the fuckin thing.

I says to her You Wally's soul mate or what?

She says to me I think that's a more apt description of *you*, Mr. D'Amato.

So I laugh and I says to her Boy, you'n Wally gotta have the snappiest fuckin pillow talk.

She wrinkles her nose and says to me Wally is my brother.

And now that she's mentionin it, they do got a resemblance. I'm about to ask her does she wanna point that gun somewhere ain't my fuckin face when I hear someone movin in the next room over what's got all the lights off.

The person comes outta that room and into this one. Showin up like they was under a black blanket got ripped away there. Shoulda figured, Wally's new place'd be burstin with shit seems like magic but ain't.

Anyway, the lady comin out from the dark room is Daff. Daphne Carr. My fuckin girl. Lookin just as fuckin swell as the last time when'd I see her, when'd she come to visit me at Sing Sing.

I smile and I says to her Hi, Daff.

She smiles back to me and says Hey, Sammy.

I says Hey, I think I fucked up, breakin outta the big house like I did.

She just nods and says Yeah, but you didn't know. Then she comes over and gives me a fuckin embrace. I smile on accounta she's so small, and I'm so big, her huggin me is like what would she look like if she was tryin to move a refrigerator by herself.

I hug her back, which is somethin a refrigerator ain't gonna do. Least, not as far as I know, only I ain't kept up with what do they got comin out at them World's Fairs.

The knob on the front door starts shakin like it's a pervert gettin off on seein me and Daff gettin close. Or else like somebody's turnin it from the outside.

Lady-Wally hisses at us Get behind me. Daff does quick, and you know what, I fuckin do too. I wanna watch Lady-Wally work on somebody ain't me.

The door opens a crack and somebody whispers Gorgonzola Integer.

Lady-Wally lowers the gun halfway and says to the door Come in.

I says to her Aw, there's a fuckin password? Nobody told me bout a fuckin password.

Then through the door comes Godric. Fuckin Godric Manfly! He's my pal what always helped me get jobs, on accounta he's the guy I know what *knows a guy,* you know what I mean. He's also my pal who'd I rough up a bit one time on accounta I thought he was stabbin my back. Only he wasn't stabbin my back, so he didn't take it kindly for a while about how'd I turn one of his feet the wrong way around. He ain't had much to do with me since that time when'd I turn one of his feet the wrong way around.

Only here he is!

I says to him Godric! How the hell are ya, old-timer? Looks like you're walkin alright!

He frowns at his ankles. The staircat comes runnin into the apartment. Then Godric slides the resta the way in and shuts the door behind him. That done, he says to me not a fuckin word, just glares.

So I says You ain't still mad about when'd I turn your foot the wrong way round, are ya? I ain't never meant I was gonna do it. And I woulda sworn I said to you sorry and all that, anyway. Ain't I done that? Ain't it water crossin the bridge when we come to it now, or what the fuck?

Godric closes his eyes and shakes his head and says I wasn't sure I was going to come tonight. Wally presented a forceful argument centered on your utility to me, professionally speaking, b-

I says to him Oh, you're too much a fuckin buffalo to get involved if you ain't wanted to. I appreciate you movin on with our fuckin get-along.

Godric sighs and looks at Daff and says Hello, Daphne.

Daff nods at him and says *I* certainly appreciate you taking time out of your night to help us brainstorm solutions here. Then she shoots a look at me says that's somethin *I* oughta said.

So I says to Godric You're a real pal, chum. And I already said to you about I'm sorry, and it looks like you're walkin alright. So let's give it a rest, huh?

Daff frowns at me a bit, then turns to Godric and says

Honestly, I'm impressed he put the word *sorry* in there at all.

Godric just smiles and rolls his eyes a bit. Which I take for kickin dirt over the bygones, or however's that sayin go.

Lady-Wally ain't listenin to this, she's busy walkin over to the window and pickin up a little mirror like Daff sometimes uses for checkin is her face on how she wants. Only Lady-Wally holds it up at the window and waves it side to side like she's pretendin it's the light on a lighthouse, and she wants a big ship what goes *honk* to watch out for these rocks already.

I says to anybody listenin So somebody wanna walk me through what'd I fuck up here, exactly? Janis was gonna bust me outta the hoosegow with paper?

Godric nods and says That's my understanding. It might have taken a number of months, but the wheels were to have been in motion as of… He looks at his watch and then he says Less than twelve hours from now. You would have been off free and clear, eventually. Wally assured me of this, and more convincingly, Janis did too.

I says No kiddin.

He says She wouldn't have made that claim if she didn't believe it to be true.

Lady-Wally nods and says Janis is really something, as far as lawyers go.

I says to Lady-Wally Yeah, I fuckin know that. And you ever gonna introduce to me your name or what?

She lowers her gun a bit more and she says to me

Ginger.

I says Okay.

The front door says to us knock, knock knock knock, knock knock, knock. Then Wally comes in, to no fuckin fanfare.

So I says at him You got a password *and* a secret fuckin knock? How come you ain't lookin to tell me bout

Godric interrupts me and says to Wally He wasn't followed, I don't think.

Wally nods and says I agree.

Ginger leans on the sill of the fuckin window and says All quiet out front.

I look at the whole operation they got here, knowin it's something what'd Wally set up. And Wally, lemme tell ya, he ain't the tread-lightly type. Most times on accounta he knows I'm treadin heavier'n he ever could not two steps behind. He one time had this whole scam goin, and I can't remember how'd it all go, but basically he figured which dumpster does he gotta dive into to get a hold of all them letters kids mail to Santa what does the post office just toss when they get em. So Wally gets em, and he sends a letter to everybody left a return address says Hey, it's me, the Post Office, I'm runnin this new thing where you send me fifty cents and I'll write your kid back like I'm Santa. Send me a buck and I'll throw in a little toy or some shit, and by the way, ask your friends do they want in on it too. He ain't wrote it just like that, but anyway, he made some serious cash off that. My point is, he ran the damn thing out of one of his apartments, put the real goddamned address as the return.

You believe that shit? So come January folks kept showin up there, on accounta Wally ain't sent them any letters, no shit, he just pocketed all that cash. Cept for some what'd he give me to spend a chilly fuckin January in that apartment, answerin the door, loomin over folks and sayin to em they got the wrong house, I ain't sent a letter in my life and do they maybe wanna get off my porch about these letters I ain't sent.

Point tellin you all that is, Wally's plannin is all about the ripoff. He don't always worry much over does he gotta protect himself or what til there's somethin *makes* him worry over it.

So if *he's* the one's settin up secret codes and knocks and wigglin mirrors while's he hidin across the street… this shit's even more serious than what'd I fuckin think about how serious is it.

The phone rings.

Wally says I think that's for you, buddy.

I look at him crosswise a bit, then go answer the phone, on accounta it's been such a screwy night thus far, it checks out the phone's gonna be for me, you know? Why not?

I pick up and I just listen.

The phone's got Janis' voice, and it says to me Shut up.

I says to her I wasn't sayin nothin.

She says *Shut up!*

I shut up on accounta she's helpin me, even though she don't like me none.

Janis growls at me I know it's not fair for me to be

angry at you for fucking this up. You didn't know. But...
goddamnit! You fucking *galoot!* What I was prepared to do
is *impossible!* Getting the *entire case* against you reopened
and thrown out! And it would have worked, too! By
means too complicated for you to even *begin* to compre-
hend, it would have worked!

I don't say nothin on accounta I figure she's only tellin
the truth. I just take my drubbin.

She says Here is what you've done, Mr. D'Amato, by
electing to break out of a *maximum security prison* to eat a
fucking *fish dinner*.

I look at Wally, makin my face into a betrayed shape,
only he just shrugs. Then Janis is thumpin again.

She fuckin continues with Instead of being out on
parole, you goddamned barbell, you're going to spend
the rest of your life as a wanted man. Your face is going
to be on posters and in papers, your name will be on the
radio and in newsreels. They're going to hunt you for the
rest of your life. Even if you leave the country, if you can
even *find* a way out, you'll either have to find a nation that
doesn't extradite, or else keep your head on a permanent
swivel. And if they ever catch you, in all likelihood, they'll
kill you.

I says Yeesh. On accounta I figured the outlook
wasn't so sunny, but that? That's fuckin midnight right
there.

I look over at Daff. She's doin a soft little smile at me.
I'm tryin to imagine a life where we ain't livin together,
on accounta I'd be bringin too much heat, riskin maybe
she goes to prison just for doin a live-along with me.

Ain't somethin I wanna think on. Ain't somethin I *can* think on, without my eyes start sweatin.

Janis is still rattlin on, she says And now *my* reputation is on the line. I've stuck my neck out for you by submitting the filings that I did, and if you've gone missing, all eyes will naturally turn to *me*. Fix this!

I says to her I just wanna say to ya, I appreciate you doin what you did with your neck, on accounta I figured you'd be some kinda sour about that time when'd I say I was gonna turn your head inside out.

Yeah, I did that too. Had a stretch there where'd I figure all the people got big hearts for me were stabbin my back. Can't remember did I tell you bout any of that, but it was a whole deal.

Janis says If you would like to make that up to me, Mr. D'Amato, then *fix this!* Then she hangs up.

I put the phone down and I says to Wally Jesus, you timed out when's she gonna call just for she gets to yell at me for half a minute?

Wally says to me Oh, she insisted.

I says She told me twice to fuckin fix it already. Which, you know, fine by me. Only, how the fuck do I do that?

Godric says That's what we're all here to figure out.

I says Tell me what do I do to fix this and I'll fuckin do it.

Daff says Right. That's the idea, Sammy.

I look at Daff and I says Ain't worth me bein outta these fuckin pajamas if I can't take you out on the town.

Daff just smiles back at me.

Wally says to me Well, that's where we have some

good news. The way we can fix this is pretty easy, actually. In principle. The details are gonna be a little squiffy, but, you know, that's why I called everybody I thought could help. We're gonna figure it out, together.

I says to him Okay, what's the way?

Wally clears his throat and says You just have to break back *in* to Sing Sing.

I'll tell ya, *squiffy* ain't the word what would I have picked to fit that.

7

I SAYS TO WALLY dot dot dot, which sounds like I'm not sayin anythin, but in my head I'm sayin dot dot dot on accounta the nothin I'm sayin's got more goin on in it than your normal nothin.

Wally just stares back at me. Can't tell is he sayin dot dot dot himself or what the fuck. Then he says What time do they wake you up in there?

So I says What time do they *wake us up?!* You mean when does the warden come shake my shoulder and say Rise and shine, sleepyhead?

He says I don't know how prison works.

I just look at him on accounta that sounds like a backdoor fuckin insult. I don't figure Wally meant it half like that, like *look at me, I ain't never been in the clink,* only I ain't in a mood's full of fuckin charity all of a sudden.

Daff sees that and, on accounta she knows all my fuckin moods and broods, she says to me We're all here to help you. We're here because we care about you.

Godric grumbles a bit, but don't say nothin crosswise.

That softens me up, what Daff said, so I says to Wally Seven in the A.M.

Wally nods and he says Alright. So that's when you need to be back in bed by. Seven in the morning.

From by the window, Lady-Wally says It's about midnight now.

I say *Ah!* on accounta I forgot she was there.

Godric says Then we have seven hours to plan and execute a break-in…at arguably *the* most notorious maximum security prison in the country.

Wally holds up his palms at Godric's tone, and he says I know, it's gonna be squiffy, but we're all intelligent people. We're all problem-solvers.

I says to Wally How long you had a sister there, Wally?

He blinks and he says What?

I point at his sister and I says You ain't never mentioned a fuckin family before.

Wally turns to *Ginger,* that's what's she called.

Ginger just smiles at him.

Wally laughs and asks me She told you she was my sister?

I just say a regular nothin this time.

He fuckin elaborates with sayin She is *not* my sister.

Ginger snaps, also ha ha gingersnaps, anyway she's by the window still (like windowsill! Vaudeville here I fuckin come), anyway again she snaps her fingers and she says You all wanna focus up? I wanna go back to bed.

Godric says Yes, let's. Then he goes over to the phone and he says I've called in a few favors with…well, it's hardly worth going in to. But I'm doing my best to acquire blueprints for Sing Sing, so we can determine where we might dig a

Daff says I'm sorry Godric, I don't mean to cut you off, but it feels like it might be useful to know… Then she turns to me and she asks How did you break *out?*

Wally snaps (eh, ain't as funny) his fingers and he says Say, that's something we should have asked earlier!

I says Ain't gonna make a difference.

So Wally says You can't just go back in the same way you came out?

I says to him No. I jumped down the windows. Third story up.

Godric says to me What does that mean, you jumped down the windows?

I hold out my arms like I'm hangin on the bars and I says to him I *jumped, down* the fuckin *windows.*

Ginger says Get a ladder.

I says to her You ever been on a fuckin ladder? You got any idea how fuckin loud those things are? Just look out the fuckin window.

Daff says to me Easy.

I says I *am* easy. I'm just sayin, breakin in's gonna be a hell of a lot harder'n breakin out.

Godric says Particularly with only seven hours to do it.

I turn to him and I says That ain't fuckin helpin, old-timer.

He says I was piggybacking off of *your* negativity!

So I says And where's that got us, huh?

Then he turns back to the phone and says Well, let's just *see* where I've gotten us with

Daff interrupts and she says Just so we don't waste time down a blind alley…does it really seem plausible we could dig an entire human-sized…er, Sammy-sized subterranean tunnel in seven hours?

Godric sighs and says Maybe closer to six, in fact. It'll take us the better part of an hour just to get up to Sing Sing.

I says to Daff You got a point about the tunnel's gotta be big, and we ain't got time. But the window ain't gonna work. Even if we got a ladder's tall enough, and we can set it up against the wall quiet enough, they got fences, and lights, and guys walkin around what're trained to blow a whistle and shout Stop that man, he's getting away! Or I figure Stop that man, he's coming back!

Wally says I bet they have guns, too.

I says Yeah, I bet they got guns.

Wally says It'd be funny if they got their gun and their whistle mixed up.

I laugh and I says Yeah, *stop that man, he's getting away!* And then I make pretend like I put a gun in my mouth and pull the trigger.

Wally laughs.

I laugh more and I says Plus the prison's called fuckin Sing Sing!

Wally laughs a little less and he says I don't get it.

I says It's just a dumb name, Sing Sing.

He says Oh, I thought you were doing wordplay or something.

I says No, I'm just sayin, it's a dumb name for a prison.

Wally's done laughin and he says Oh. Gotcha.

Godric's still standin there with the phone in his hand, watchin us with all the veins in his face pokin out against the skin, like how nipples do through your shirt when it's cold out.

Daff says Six hours, gentlemen.

So I nod to her, and to Godric I says Look, we ain't gotta go score no fuckin blueblocks or what'd you say. I can make em myself. Then I go find a piece of paper. Wally asks me You mind not drawing on that one? So I says to him Fine, what can I draw on? He gets me another piece of paper and says You can draw on this one. And what's more, he hands me a fuckin pen with it. So then I get to drawin the whole of fuckin Sing Sing what I got in my head. All the fuckin floors, halls, doors, every piece of fuckin layout I got stored away. Scratchin out my *own* blueblocks, with my *own* fuckin intel.

I never figured it was intel I got, on accounta it takes a fuckin objective to turn useless bullshit into intel. Mess hall's got six windows. There's a dumb fact. Who gives a shit? Well, maybe we wanna climb in the mess hall windows. Whaddyaknow, now it's intel.

I put one last fuckin swipe on it and show it to em. They look at me like they can't even believe how'd this bruiser draw this fuckin thing.

I says to em Some of this, I'm just assumin on. The other wards, I'm figurin they're just about the same as where were they puttin me up in C ward. Otherwards, or *wise,* I'm sayin...this is the fuckin thing.

Ginger points to one of the walls and says What is this supposed to be?

I says to her That's the fuckin wall what faces the river.

She says No, I mean...is this supposed to be the prison?

Wally and Janis look up at me all waitfully, like they was wonderin the very same, only they knew better'n to say so.

I look down at my work of fuckin art, then back at Ginger, and I says to her Course it's the fuckin prison. You ain't never seen a prison top-down before? It's top-down.

She asks me So Sing Sing is a parallelogram?

I tell her Course it ain't, it's a fuckin penitentiary. Would you fuckin keep up? I look at Wally like I'm askin *Where the hell'd you find this lady?*

Real quiet, Wally tells my map You, uh, it doesn't *look* as though Sing Sing has any doors. According to your representation.

So I ask him What'm I puttin in the doors for, we can't fuckin use em. Less you want I'm gonna walk in and say to em Don't mind me, just back from takin my fuckin postprandial?

Godric adds It also looks like there's a giant fried egg in the middle of it.

I says A what? Then I look at where's he pointin and I says That was fuckin artistic license. It's *top-down.*

He asks me So it doesn't actually correspond to anything. Without a fuckin question mark, he asks me that.

I shrug and says You one of those people goes to the pictures and complains everythin ain't just-so?

He says If there were dire stakes attending those inaccuracies, such as you are now facing, then yes, I would.

So I throw my hands up and I says to him Alright, since you're the fuckin art critic how bout you scribble a better fuckin Sing Sing?

He picks the phone back up to his face and says to me I was working on just that, after a fashion!

Wally says We're all on the same side here, Samuzzo.

Ginger says That's not really a critic's job, to produce a superior piece of art.

Daff says We're losing the thread a bit here, huh?

Godric says I'm trying to get the blueprints!

So I says The blueprints ain't gonna help! They got lights and fences and guys and gates and dogs, and I don't see how the fuck am I gonna get back into my cell from the outside, so I gotta get back *in* the fuckin lockup without anybody seein and then how the fuck am I gonna get back in my cell on accounta the door to it's still locked, and also we got six fuckin hours to figure this out! So Daff's right, let's get the fuckin thread and get to sewin this up!

Then I look over my map and I says Alright, which wall did I say is the one's near the river?

Everybody says Uuuuugh.

8

HALF-HOUR IN we got fuckin nothin to show for the minutes. You wanna slice off the time's gotta go to gettin upstate, which Godric is real fuckin keen on, we got five and a half hours left prior to the clink cops pop a head in and wonder where'd Samuzzo's window get to, and how come's he made of plaster paper now.

Then I remember I got another problem I gotta worry about.

I says Shit.

Everybody says to me What. They says it in a tone of voice ain't puffin me up with fuckin optimisms on are we gonna work out the first fuckin problem.

I says to em I gotta go see Tear's people.

Wally asks me At this hour?

Godric asks me Who?

Daff don't say nothin, she's just frownin at the fuckin ceilin.

So I explain to em how Tear's the guy faked he was havin a fuckin medical event to help get me outta the hoosegow, and how'd I tell him I was gonna check in on his people as a thank ya.

Wally shakes his head and he says Sammy, that's real noble of ya, but we don't really have time for noble.

Godric talks over him and says Why would you need to check in on them?

I says On accounta I said I would.

He asks me Are they suddenly in peril? *Tonight,* are they in peril?

I says to him The fuck do I know? I just said to him I'd check in on em after I got out.

Wally says You still can. After you get back in, and then get out again.

Then Ginger says Besides, going to see them will only make for more witnesses who can testify to your having broken out.

I says to em Raheeq's already seen me. There was an old-timer in a truck, and the cab guy, only he figured I'm somebody ain't me. But so what, I'm supposed to fuckin splat those three just on accounta they seen me? I'm supposed to do three murders now?

Ginger shakes her head and says I didn't say anything like that.

I says to her You're holdin a gun!

She looks down at it like she's gotta double check what'd I say, then she says So what?

I says You tell me!

She says What?

Daff says Hey.

I says to Daff What? in a tone what ain't the one I just used at Ginger.

Daff says to me I have an idea.

I says to her Shoot. Then I look at Ginger and I says to her Not you, with the gun. I ain't sayin shoot to you.

Ginger narrows her eyes at me and says I'm here to be lookout for *you,* asshole.

I narrow my eyes right back at her and I says That's a good point. I got no idea why am I behavin the way I am at you.

Ginger just stares at me like she can't figure out what's goin on with my words ain't bein said in a way matches what am I sayin.

Godric says I'm enormously interested in hearing Daphne's idea. He says it in a way sounds like he means it, which, you know, he fuckin better.

We all look at Daff.

She scratches at her chin some and then she says This might be a ridiculous idea, but…what if we stage a break-out?

Seems like her voice runs a few laps around the room, til it gets tired and just sorta goes away like how voices do.

I says to her You wanna break Tear out? Or who?

She shakes her head and she says to me I don't want to break anyone out. But my thought is…maybe, we try to make it *look* like we're breaking someone out. Go in with force, maybe knock down a wall or…I don't know. That's a little dramatic. But…sound and fury, something distracting. We use that as a diversion, during which we sneak you in, Sammy. Make it look convincing – don't hurt anybody, of course, but really sell it. Then let the guards chase us off. They'll feel good about themselves, which'll hopefully make them complacent.

Her voice ain't got as much room to run around when's she done talkin there, on accounta everybody's thinkin so loud.

Godric says Let's assume we adopt that approach, and succeed. All we'll have accomplished is returning Samuzzo to the interior of the prison, but *not* to the inside of his cell. Which is, crucially, where he needs to be.

Wally says He could just say he was never *in* his cell. When they did lockup, he could say he was in the bathroom, using the bathroom.

I says to Wally You ain't gonna believe this, but the johns in Sing Sing are fuckin en suite.

Wally says Oh.

I says And anyway, I said Evenin to Skip. He seen me in my cell after lockup.

Daff shrugs and says It was an idea.

Wally thinks on that and he says That's not half bad, though.

Godric does a little unhappy burp noise like he figures it's at *least* half bad. But he don't say nothin.

Wally says If we can get you back into the prison, Sammy, and then your only problem is, oh, hey, there's a lock on my cell door...locks were made to be picked. *Any* lock can be picked. I can teach you to pick a lock.

Ginger says How fast can you teach him? Because it's gonna take some time to figure out how to do a *break-out* at *Sing Sing*. And we've only got five hours and change.

I says Plus I gotta go check on Tear's people.

Godric puts his forehead into his hands and he says This is madness.

Ginger asks Wally How long will it take you to teach him to pick a lock?

Wally shrugs and says Ten minutes. Twenty, tops.

Daff asks him That's it?

I says to Wally I don't figure that's the right number. On accounta it don't come natural to me, I'm doin somethin with my fingers what ain't makin a fist.

Ginger snorts. Looks at Daff.

Daff waves her off like Forget about it.

I'm about to ask the fuck are they snortin about when Wally says Alright, an hour and a half.

Daff asks Could you teach him in the car? On the way to Sing Sing?

Wally asks Who's driving?

She says Say it's neither of you.

Wally says No, I couldn't. We'd need a door. I don't know why I asked who was driving.

Godric says That raises a worthwhile question: who, exactly, would be performing this mock break-out? Then he waves his arms around the room and he says None of us, certainly.

Ginger says I'm happy to drive.

Daff says You probably wouldn't need too many people, would you? I don't think you'd want more than can fit in a single car, at least.

Wally looks at Godric and he says If this question is out of order then slap me silly, but isn't finding muscle for jobs exactly your wheelhouse?

Godric says It is, ordinarily. When the parameters are clear, as far as the objectives and the pay, and, critically, when there is sufficient time to plan. Then he picks his nose up like a dog smellin a pork chop two counties over and he says I have a professional reputation that I do not mean to compromise with an operation as slapdash and, I am sorry to say, likely to fail as this one.

Daff says Come on, Godric.

He pouts his lips and crinkles his forehead. Weird thing to do with a face, I gotta say. Then *he* says I'm sorry to say it. I'm here to help, of course, but…I have to safeguard my own prospects, you understand.

Wally says to him When you think about it, Sammy is

I interrupt him and I says I'm not takin nothin personalwise here.

That ain't all the way true, only I'm feelin some kinda generous on accounta I just had my own fuckin whatabout in my head go off. And Godric's gotta be the one's gonna help me out with it.

So I says to him, I says I got a whatabout for ya.

Godric says nothin in a way says he's listenin.

I says You figure Chet's still up at this hour?

Wally says Uuuuuuh you mean Chet Crowder, Sammy?

I nod at him up and down.

Daff says Doesn't he run the, um…

I says to her Yeah. Then I look at the clock and I says Bet he's doin one now, point of fuckin fact. They go late.

Ginger looks at how's everybody frownin about my suggestion, and she says Who's this? Chet Crowder?

Godric blinks real slow, and turns his head at Ginger real slow, and he says to her at a normal speed Chet Crowder. He runs a sort of…therapeutic support group for hired muscle. Called Paci-FIST.

Daff says I feel like the problem is in the name there.

Isn't their whole schtick that members are expected to have put their bruising days behind them? I mean… aren't they all pacifists?

I says to her Yeah.

She looks at me like What the fuck.

I says to her They're still locomotive-sized fellas, though. And we ain't plannin to hurt nobody there. Long as they ain't gonna get squeamish about really lettin the infrastructure have it, I don't see no issue with they ain't lookin to throw a punch.

Godric don't look too happy, but he sighs and says I can give him a call.

I says Alright. We got a plan.

Everybody just stares at me.

I says to em again Alright. We got a plan.

Daff says It sounded like you were going to review everyone's roles.

I think about that and I says That ain't *my* role. I'm the one gets *told* what's my role, typicalwise.

Godric says Nothing about this is typical. So I think your role this time is to review the roles.

I says to him *Now* we're talkin. Then I look at everybody as I says to em what the fuck are they doin, I says to em Wally, you're gonna drive me to go see Tear's people real quick. Godric, you give Chet a call, see is he up and does he got any big buddies wanna go in on the fake-out break-out. Ginger, you sit tight til we're gonna need you behind the wheel up to Sing Sing. Daff, you go home and read a good book.

Don't nobody say nothin crosswise to what'd I say.

Which is a weird fuckin feelin, lemme tell ya. Tellin folks what to do. Unless it's me tellin em Here's what's gonna happen or Lemme know where the money is, that ain't my role, like what'd I say to everybody just a second ago.

But turns out I got it in me to give the roles out every now and then. Huh! Go fuckin figure.

9

WALLY SAYS TO ME Get down, so I Get down. Only I'm too big to fit in the foot-spot in his fuckin jalopy, so I figure who-ever's drivin by's gonna see the top of my fuckin coconut still.

But what the fuck, I get down and I ask him Cops?

He squints and he says Oh. I thought so. Maybe not.

I push myself back up into my seat and I says Your fuckin footspot don't smell so swell.

Wally just shrugs and says to me In my defense, it's not a spot where people are supposed to put their noses.

I says to him You told me I oughta put my nose there.

He says to me That was because I thought I saw the cops.

We drive on for a while, then he says to me Did you ever tell me the address of where we're going?

I says to him Not that I can fuckin recall did I do that or not.

He says Oh. So where am I going right now?

I says I got no fuckin idea. I figured *you* knew.

He says Oh, nope. Not if you didn't tell me the address.

So I says to him the address what'd Tear tell me.

He laughs and says Glad I asked, eventually! Then turns the car around so's it's goin the other fuckin way.

We go on that way for a while, then I says Maybe what if we actually broke Tear out? You think he'd go for that or what?

Wally says You'd know better than I would. I've never met the guy.

I says I think he might be in for a whole lifetime.

Wally says Gosh. What'd he do?

I says Crimes, I figure.

He says Oh, yeah. Do you know which ones?

I says to him Nothin bad, I don't figure. None of the pants-off crimes, I know that much. Word gets around, bout fellas what done the pants-off crimes.

He says to me He sounds like a decent enough guy.

So I says I'm just thinkin, you know…long as we're fakin a break-out, maybe we might as well go and do one? As a fuckin thank you to he helped *me* out.

Wally says That's a real nice thought to have, Sammy. But that's just got *me* thinking, you know, maybe he doesn't *want* that. Just in terms of what it means to live as a fugitive, you know. For all the reasons you don't want to live as a fugitive. You know.

I says Yeah, but he ain't got the option of Janis is gonna get him free and clear with papers.

Wally says I hear you on that. But, you know, that's a lot more risk for you and Chowder's g-uh, Crowder's guys, not Chowder.

I says Chet Crowder.

Wally nods and says It's just a lot more risk for you guys. And if Tear doesn't wanna get broken out, and you end up getting pinched because of the extra risk you took on, to *break* him out, that'd stink.

I shrug and I says Alright, it was a bad fuckin idea. I was just thinkin.

Wally says Oh, come on now, I think it was a terrific idea. Just didn't quite gibe with the hand we've been dealt.

I says to him I ain't never seen you play the hand what'd you get dealt in your life.

Wally says Well if you put cards up your sleeves or in your socks or down your briefs ahead of time, the way I see it, that counts as having been dealt those cards. Metaphorically speaking.

I says I don't figure the croupiers' union's gonna sign off on that.

Wally shrugs and says I've never brought it up to them.

I ask him You figure croupiers got their own union?

He says I'd be surprised if they did.

I says Then how come you said you ain't never brought it up to them, like they got a union?

He says I was just going with what you said.

I fold my arms and says Well anyway, I don't figure we oughta break Tear outta Sing Sing without we fuckin ask does he want us to break him out or not.

Wally says I'd sign off on that.

I sniff and I says Could be we give him the high sign though, huh? Could be he's some kinda helpful from the inside.

Wally says I guess that's possible. Anything's possible.

I fold my arms tighter so's the forearms start flexin, which pushes em back apart on accounta the muscles are pretty fuckin big. I ain't sayin that boastwise, just statin the fuckin facts. I tell him What do you figure for the odds we get hitched tryin to pull this shit off?

Wally's quiet for a while there.

I says to him Hitched like our plan hits a fuckin hitch. Catches on a hitch. Whatever the fuck.

Wally laughs and he says I was gonna say. Pretty low, I'd put the odds of us getting hitched.

I don't laugh and I says I ain't fuckin goofin here, Wally. Lookin at this shit with your readin glasses on, you figure we're gonna get me back in my fuckin cell, in six and some hours?

Wally says Five and some, actually. We're gonna lose an hour to the drive.

I says to him I figure I'm just keepin the drive time on the clock tick.

He says As long as we don't forget that's included.

I says to him Alright, whatever number'd you just say, that's how much we got, timewise. You figure this is comin off? On accounta if it ain't…maybe I oughta use them hours as a jump on gettin me and Daff outta town.

Wally says You might have to go further than just out of town.

I says I'm real fuckin clear on that, Wally.

Wally nods for a bit.

I says to him Ain't likin the quiet there.

He says Just trying to think it through.

I says to him You're such a fuckin sunnysider, far as the can-we-do-it, I ain't likin the quiet.

Wally says It's gonna be tough, Sammy, for sure. No doubt about that.

I says to him But.

He says But what?

I says That's what the fuck *I* wanna know.

He says Huh?

I says I'm waitin for you to say *But,* and then somethin puts a big fuckin smile on my fuckin face, far as are we gonna get fully fucked on this or not. I'm some kinda hopeful we've got Crowder's guys're gonna help from out here. Could be Tear helps us out from inside. You're so good with the fuckin scams and flimflams all over. That's a team, right? We got a fuckin chance here, or don't we, is what I just want you to fuckin say to me now.

Wally says to me The way I see it, Sammy, we've just gotta try.

You better fuckin believe that rearranges my face. Only it ain't into any kinda way might get called a smile.

10

T EAR'S PLACE ain't too far away, just up in Washington Heights. Wasn't too long ago the Heights still had fuckin trees all over it, and since the Rockefeller place burned down it's lookin like how do we know the trees ain't makin a comeback. Whole neighborhood's rotten with fuckin Irish folks now, too. I ain't got a fuckin prejudice about that, some of my best friends is Irish. Which ones, I couldn't tell ya off the top of my head. Gotta figure it's the one's ain't never said no to a slug of booze, even after they turned from pink to yellow. I ain't sayin all the Irish are fuckin alcoholics just on accounta their heritage. I'm just sayin all alcoholics are Irish.

Anyway, I'm some kinda surprised Tear's livin up with the heel-clickers on accounta he's a color ain't pink. That don't bother me none; I ain't worried about what color is a fella's skin. I only mention what color is this fuckin guy on accounta the Irish and the Blacks, they ain't known for the fuckin Kum-Ba-Ya with each other, so I'm wonderin are they askin to borrow a cup of sugar at gunpoint or what. But like I was sayin, colors and creeds ain't part of my lookout. Some of those paddies back home, these goofy little sing-song motherfuckers, they ain't gettin along so swell on accounta they got their own prejudices. At each *other*. You ain't sayin the right sortsa prayers, fuckin hi-diddle-oh, in the dirt you go. What's goin on there, right? Life ain't about holdin your own hand and mumblin about Please make my boss give me a raise or some shit. Life's about doin jobs for money until you die.

But would you quit crankin me up about the Irish already? Tear's a Black, Wally's a Jew, I'm normal. It ain't a big deal one way or the other, long as ain't none of us

Irish.

Wally's parkin the car and I says to him Hey Wally.

He don't answer right away on accounta he's parkin the car, and the way he does it you'd figure it for a fuckin full contact sport.

Then he finishes parkin the car so I says to him again Hey Wally.

He looks at me and says Don't worry.

I says to him What am I don't worryin about?

He says If this all goes sideways, I'll look after Daphne.

I says to him The fuck does she need you lookin at her for?

He says *After,* not at.

I says to him She's got a fuckin job. She ain't gonna starve.

Wally shrugs like *Guess I'm a moron for sayin what'd I say,* then he opens his door and gets outta the car.

I yell out at him You wanna give her walkin around money for no reason though, I don't figure she'll spit on your shoes about it. Then I get outta the car too.

He says Sounds like she's doing alright for herself.

I tell him I appreciate you sayin you're gonna give her an allowance, but she's doin alright for herself.

He says That's what it sounds like.

I'm walkin towards the steps what go into Tear's people's buildin. Wally starts followin. It ain't till we're movin like so that I take note of this ain't hardly ever the way it goes. Most time I'm loomin behind *him,* or followin *him.* It's fuckin nice, bein in front for once, lemme tell ya.

I says to him Hey Wally, if this all goes sidewise, who's gonna look after *you?*

Wally says How do you mean?

I says to him You're always doin all them scams don't go quite how'd you figure they'd go.

Wally says That's right.

I says to him Most times it ain't a problem they don't go how'd you figure on accounta you got me loomin behind ya, punchin my fist when I gotta.

Wally says That's just how it goes, most times.

So I says But if you ain't got me loomin behind ya, and the scam don't go quite how'd ya figure, who's gonna keep ya from gettin dangled off a rooftop by your ankles?

I can hear Wally walkin a little bit slower, til he says Well jeez, I hadn't really thought about that.

Now we're up the stairs and I knock on the door's got the number on it what Tear told me means it's his people's place. The number on the door's Three, if you're the kinda person's gotta know what's the fuckin number on the door.

Wally says We'll just need to make sure this all goes well, then.

I says to him Great fuckin idea, Wally. I'm kickin myself for I didn't think of that earlier, that we oughta make sure it all goes well.

The door with the Three on it opens.

And I don't say nothin for a minute.

I ain't kiddin neither, gotta be near to a whole fuckin minute I don't say nothin.

Then I says The fuck are you doin here?

Tear says to me Having a late dinner. You hungry?

I don't say nothin. On accounta he's meant to be locked up in fuckin Sing Sing.

He says to me Thanks for coming, by the way. My boys didn't think you'd come through, but I knew. They're on their way now.

Wally asks me Hey Sammy, who's this guy?

I says This is Tear. The guy what helped bust me outta the big house.

Wally says Oh. You didn't mention he broke out with you.

I says to Wally, only I'm still lookin at Tear while I'm talkin, I says to Wally I didn't fuckin figure he did.

Tear just smiles at me. Big friendly smile on this fuckin guy.

Wally asks me So…what's going on?

I says to Wally, still lookin at Tear, I says I figure I got fuckin played.

Tear's smile gets bigger, but stays the same kinda friendly.

MISE EN PLACE: CHET

THE WHOLE BRANZINO

THE **HARDEST PART** of running a Paci-FIST meeting wasn't getting the guys to talk, or keeping them from fighting. This wasn't exactly the sort of support group to which one could be court-ordered, after all; the men who came here did so because they wanted to be here. Because they wanted to be heard – and, at times begrudgingly, to listen. Except only *rarely* begrudgingly, because they all knew that no one else was going to take their problems seriously. Most people, the ordinary citizens, they look at hulking, scarred muscle-for-hire of the sort which constitutes the rank and file of Paci-FIST, and feel only fear. Or perhaps those with especially deep pockets see opportunity. The point, though, is that they see a *tool*, a weapon they can either wield, or that might be wielded against them.

Which was why Chet Crowder had started Paci-FIST. He and his fellow bruisers and enforcers, the men who wore tight suits and stood behind the boss while they made this or that deal to control this or that enterprise in this or that territory, the instruments by which someone else's grand designs were realized...they needed somewhere they could leave the thankless business of head-busting at the door, and begin to wonder: what do *I* hope to get out of life? Who am *I*, when the job is over and there's nobody left to menace? What size suit do *I* really want to wear?

Much to Chet's astonishment, the sorts of men most people thought of as *goons* were fairly game for such self-affirming rumination. The hardest part of running these meetings, then, was getting these men to ask the big questions without simply agreeing with everything Chet or anyone else offered that sounded remotely like an answer. After all, nearly to a man, they had worked for vain, ambitious, emotionally impulsive criminal kingpins, not the sorts of fellows one got far in second-guessing. Best to just cackle along with whatever little jokes they made, or crack your knuckles after they threatened somebody, maybe sprinkle in a few chestnuts like "you got that right, boss," or "I was thinkin the same thing, only dumber."

Good habits all, for making it through the day whilst employed by one of the Families, or Syndicates, to say nothing of the deceptively named Friendship Societies. But habits best left at the door, for a Paci-FIST meeting.

Also to be left at the door: belligerence. Which most

of the guys got, intuitively, from the name of the group. Granted, Chet might have been too clever by half in drawing attention to the third syllable – FIST – mixed messages and all that, but hey. *Most* people got it. Which made peacekeeping only the *second* most difficult part of running the meetings.

Oh, but tonight was shaping up to be an especially long night; he was getting pings on both the first and second major difficulties. The first from Robb, who'd started coming just two weeks ago, but had yet to speak until tonight. Thus far, all he'd managed to volunteer was that he worked for Gavaroli, and that he was coming in response to something specific he'd been forced to do in that man's employ. This thing had so disturbed him, he was now contemplating hanging up his metaphorical hat for good. He'd yet to get around to explicating just what that specific something had been, though.

"So," Chet once more coaxed, feeling a bit like a tone-deaf snake charmer, "this was something you were forced to do quite recently, then?"

"That's right," Robb replied reflexively, *"real* recently, yeah."

"Please, you don't need to agree with everything I'm saying."

Robb nodded furiously, then crossed his hands over his lap and gave a booming cackle. His eyes bulged, and he shook his head a few times. "Sorry," he said. "Old habits, boss. *Chet."*

"There are no bosses here."

"You got that right." Another cackle. *"Shoot,* boss, I'm

sorry. Boss. *Chet!*"

"Just fucking skip him," Gephen insisted.

Chet raised an eyebrow in Gephen's direction; he'd had problems with that one before, and suspected he was going to have still more tonight. Of all the times difficulty number two had arisen in a meeting of late, nearly a full quarter of those incidents could be lain at Gephen's outrageously large feet. The story was he'd grown up with none other than Paolo Bucchinati, had never been far from that fearsome man's flank in all that time – was, Chet had heard it argued, more responsible for Bucchinati's stranglehold on liquor importation than the man himself was. The gruesome stories Gephen told in these meetings, of flayings and dismemberments and just generally turning live human bodies into anatomy textbook diagrams, weren't even the worst Chet had heard of him. But it was inimical to the spirit of Paci-FIST to bar a man's entry based on what he had done; this group was all about who he could *become*, after all.

Still, Chet found it a challenge to take Gephen at his word, that those days were behind him. Indeed, he wondered why the bastard even came to these things.

No. Not a bastard. It wasn't right to judge people, Chet upbraided himself. Who was he to judge? Just a man. They were all just men. Large, muscular men.

"Now hang on," Chet said to Gephen. "It's Robb's turn to speak. When it's *your* turn to speak, no one interrupts. And now it's *Robb's* turn t-"

"I'm saying maybe it shouldn't be his turn anymore," Gephen interrupted. "I'm saying, maybe we should skip him."

Yeah, a few of the men sitting in the circle of chairs agreed, *there's an idea, maybe we skip him.*

Chet took a deep breath and shook his head. "No. It's his turn. We'll give him as much time as he needs."

That's right, the circle muttered, in some of the same voices, *as much time as he needs, he's gonna get it alright.*

After a few more moments glaring at Gephen, Chet turned back to Robb. "If you're comfortable sharing, we would all like to hear what it was you did, that brought you here, to our meeting."

Robb nodded. "Oh, I'm comfortable sharing. I'm *real* comfortable." He cracked his knuckles and his neck, then paused and made a confused face at the far wall.

"Alright," Gephen grunted, slapping his thighs and rising to his feet, "he's forfeit his turn. *I* want to go."

"Gephen," Chet tutted, "please retake your seat." Chet turned to Thomas, easily Paci-FIST's least physically imposing member. "Would you feel comfortable yielding your turn today to Gephen, with the understanding that you would speak first next week?"

Thomas shrugged. "Suits me fine."

"Thank you, Thomas." Chet turned back to Gephen. "Will that work for you? If you speak next, once Robb had finished h-"

"Robb's done talking," Gephen snapped. He leered in the relative newcomer's direction. "Aren't you, Robb?"

"You're not, Robb," Chet encouraged. "Not if you don't want to be, you're not."

Robb glanced nervously from Gephen to Chet, back

and forth, back and forth. "I...don't know?"

Chet smiled. "That's a kind of progress, isn't it?"

"Whatever you say, boss."

Gephen laughed. "What a mook!"

Chet frowned at him, but said nothing. Passing judgment on another man's predisposition to pass judgment was simply more judgment. Which was illustrative of how retributive cycles could form. The only enlightened choice was to break the chain, introduce a modicum of compassion and magnanimity.

In short, Chet didn't think it would be a good look to kick Gephen out of the group. Officially, he *couldn't*; organizer and meeting leader though he was, Paci-FIST was technically a leaderless organization. In point of fact, though, Chet absolutely could punt Gephen from the group, if he wanted. But he didn't want, for the optics. Which was a shame; he'd more or less written the man off as a lost cause. Not something he enjoyed doing, writing a man off like that, but there it was.

Louie, who seemed to have appointed himself Chet's sidekick without having ever consulted him, whispered to Chet "do you want me to *make* him sit?"

He didn't whisper anywhere near quietly enough.

"Beg pardon?" Gephen snapped. He cupped a hand behind his right ear and pointed it directly at Louie. "What was that, boy?"

"I'm not a *boy,"* Louie sulked, looking to Chet to confirm that point.

"Aaaaalright," Chet announced. "Perhaps you *should* share what's agitating you, Gephen. With an eye towards a Ring of Resolution between the two of us?"

Gephen shook his head. "I'm fucking not doing a Ring."

"You've been resistant to our various self-investigative techniques. And yet, you continue to attend these meetings. Why is that, Gephen?"

"For the fucking company," Gephen grinned.

Chet studied Gephen carefully, searching for the truth behind his perfect attendance record, beneath that mask he called a face.

He had the chilling suspicion that there was little more to Gephen than his mask.

"Chet!" called a voice from the kitchen. Or maybe it was the radio room; they were holding this week's meeting at Louie's place. *Much* closer to New York than Chet's home in Connecticut, which gave Louie's a real convenience factor for most of these guys, but god golly was the floor plan here strange.

He started. "Yes?"

Johnthan (*no A in the middle*, he was always careful to point out) poked his head out of the kitchen, waving the receiver of the phone at shoulder-level.

Chet cocked an eyebrow. "For me?" He looked to Louie.

Louie looked just as confused as Chet felt. Who was calling for him here at Louie's? Which was to say, who knew he *was* here? The meetings were meant to be a well-kept secret amongst bruisers...

Ignoring the popping of his knees, Chet rose to standing and exited the circle. "Telephone," he announced flatly, patting Robb encouragingly on the shoulder as he left.

He took the phone from Johnthan, nodded gratefully, then cranked his neck to hold it between his right cheek and shoulder. "Who is this?" he asked.

"It's Godric Manfly," a familiar voice on the other end announced. "Bit late for a meeting, isn't it?"

Still unused to phone etiquette, Chet nodded, nearly losing his grip on the phone in the process. He caught it as it fell, and returned it to his ear in a tightly bunched fist. "I'm curious as to how you knew to call *here,* Godric, as opposed to my home."

"Nothing magic. Ear to the ground. You know."

"Hm. Interesting." He threw a quick look at the Paci-FISTers (oh, they needed to brainstorm a better thing to call themselves than that) in Louie's living room, then let the curly-cue cord of the phone reel him into...wow, a *billiards* room, how unexpected. Louie really was doing well for himself, huh? Good for him. "Well Godric, I confess to being a bit apprehensive to take your call. As the last time we spoke, you introduced Samuzzo D'Amato into my life, just before he ran full-tilt into a whole whirlwind of legal woes."

"My understanding had been that you facilitated something of a breakthrough for him."

"Oh, of course. That's what we do here. I'm more thinking about personal proximity to police activity. That's something we all try to avoid, you understand."

"That's something everybody tries to avoid."

"Indeed. I bring that up simply to explain my apprehension, as I ask you: in regards to what are you calling?"

"Samuzzo D'Amato."

"Who is in prison now, yes?"

"Well…sort of."

"…are you asking me to assist on any kind of break-out?"

"Sort of."

"You cannot break a man out of Sing Sing. It's impossible."

"We don't want to break him out. We want to break him back *in.*"

"…"

"He already broke out. We want to break him back in. But we're planning to make the break-in look like a break-out. But it'll actually be a break-*in.*"

"…"

"And we have about five hours to plan and execute this."

Chet lifted a hand to his forehead and kneaded his brow. "Did he hurt any of the guards?"

"What?"

"When he was breaking out."

"Oh. No. He says he didn't."

Another Paci-FIST success story, Chet reflected, before chastening himself for the personal pride he took in someone else's accomplishment. "Good for him."

"Yes, yes, good for him. Except not really. If he has to spend the rest of his life as a fugitive, I imagine there'll be more than a few scenarios in which he's forced to hurt someone to protect himself. Eliminating unfriendly witnesses, that sort of thing."

Chet kneaded harder, faster. "Aaah...I suspect you may be right there." He took a deep breath and lowered his hand. "So why, I wonder, are you calling *me* about this? Your reputation positions you as the center of a massive web of association and debts of honor. Yet I hardly know you, and owe you nothing. So why call me?"

"Because *honor* isn't a word I'd use for most of the people I know. Except you. I trust you, Chet. Your competence, your integrity, and your discretion. Those are the qualities I need right now."

Chet treated himself to a few more seconds of forehead kneading.

"I know you were the right man to call," Godric continued, "because you still haven't asked me what's in this for you."

Chet chewed on the inside of his cheek, then said "is there a plan in place?"

"Loosely."

"How many men does it require?"

"Somewhere between three and five."

"And you would need us immediately?"

"The sooner the better."

Chet nodded. "Okay."

And so they made more plans.

At the conclusion of which, Godric reiterated, in a slightly more incredulous tone, "you still haven't asked me what's in this for you."

Chet smiled. "Just as you clearly haven't asked *yourself* what's in this for me." With that, he hung up. Feeling downright mischievous, with regard to his parting line. In truth, Chet didn't want anything out of this. He believed strongly that tendering aid to those in need was its own reward. And if this happened to redound positively on his reputation amongst the tri-state area's bruisers, and if this happened to give him a chit with D'Amato to call in at a later date…well, Chet wouldn't turn his nose up at any of that.

He returned to Louie's living room.

Being big, he was sure the Paci-FISTers would agree, had its advantages, but quietly scrambling back into seats after piling up near a doorway to eavesdrop on a phone call was not one of them.

They all returned to their seats with the grace and composure of cannonballs.

Thomas, who had his own complicated history with D'Amato, didn't bother to pretend he hadn't had a sneaky little listen: "Did I hear you say 'Samuzzo D'Amato'?"

Chet nodded, then relayed all that Godric had told him, all they had planned together.

Gephen blinked, astounded. "And you want us to just…go help him?"

"Right now?" Robb wondered.

"It's only thirty minutes or so into the city," Louie offered lamely.

"What's the pay?" Gephen demanded.

"Yeah," Johnthan echoed. "I'm trying to save up for a, uh, something."

Chet ignored the uneasy chattering. "No pay. This is

doing a nice thing for a fellow Paci-FISTer. As we would do for any of you, should you find yourselves in a fix. This is part of the mission, gentlemen."

Within five minutes, almost everyone had left. The only men to stay behind were Chet, Louie, Johnthan, Thomas, and, incredibly, Gephen.

Thomas refused to sit on anybody's lap, so they had to take two cars.

STEP TWO:
READY THE FISH

THE WHOLE BRANZINO

1

TURNS OUT, soon as I told Tear about does he wanna help me fly the coop or what, he starts thinkin on maybe he wants to start flappin his own wings. He ain't fixin to tell me the hows and the whatnots, for reasons I ain't so fuckin fond of, but gimme a fuckin minute and I'll get there, I gotta get you *here* firstwise.

So back in Sing Sing, when I says to Tear Tonight's the night, he goes to *his* buddies and says Tonight's the night. This whole thing about him havin a fuckin family? He ain't got a fuckin family. He's just tellin me somethin's gonna get me to his place, on accounta he figures once I'm here and he's sayin the words Two hundred thousand dollars to me, I ain't gonna find it within myself to head back down the fuckin stairs without I ask some follow-ups.

I ask him How come you ain't just said to me Let's why don't you and I finagle our breakout on equal fuckin terms, on accounta I got a job's got a spot for ya?

He gets us some fuckin moonshine or *somethin's* got a punch, and he says I didn't think about breaking out until you asked me to help you do it. I didn't even really think about it being *possible*. So that got me thinking…but by the time I started planning this job, getting my boys on the legwork, that sort of thing, you were already well on your way with your plan. I thought it could only complicate things, telling you about *my* plan.

I says to him Things ain't exactly feelin so easy to me right now.

Wally takes a sip of whatever'd Tear hand him and he just about chokes on it. Starts makin a *haa haa haa* noise like he took a bite outta some pizza what's fresh from the hotbox.

Tear put his glass down and picks up some papers off the table by the window. He shuffles through em and he says to me This is our freedom, man. *True* freedom.

I says to him Quit shakin your papers, I can't see what do they say.

He keeps shakin his papers at me and he says Listen, we hit this bank, there's enough money in that vault to let us all just…vanish. *Tonight*. Rich as Croesus and living the life for at least a decade.

While's he flickin through the pages, I can see he's got fuckin blueprints. *Real* ones. Nothin what'd nobody scribble on a fuckin placemat.

Fuck me. He wants to rob a fuckin bank.

THE WHOLE BRANZINO

I says to him You put some kinda fuckin plannin into this, huh?

Tear nods and he says We can do it. It's never been done before, which is precisely why we can do it. A prison break and a bank robbery in one night!

Wally gets himself back into fuckin control from the beverage, and he says I don't know about this, fellas. Even if you had enough time to do the heist – and I think it is more of a heist than a robbery, since to me

Tear interrupts him and says It's a bank robbery.

Wally says For sure, but I just, when I hear robbery, I'm thinking there are people you point your gun at and say Stick Em Up, whereas you'd be going into a closed bank after hours, so there won't be anybody there to stick anything up, no matter how hard you point your gun.

I says to Wally Could be there's a night guy.

Wally says That's a good point. He'd be able to Stick Em Up. But whoever's there, though, I don't think we'd be able to get Sammy back up to the prison in time to

Tear interrupts and he asks Wally Why the fuck would we take him back to the prison?

Wally says Oh, then he explains the whole what's-up quick as can be.

Tear does some funny stuff with his eyebrows, then he says Well, that's just it. Pull the bank job and you won't *need* to go back. That was my whole thinking in bringing you in on this now, is, this is your ticket to freedom! I've arranged a ferry to take us to

I says to him Oh, no. These fuckin ferries're never

goin where do you figure they're goin.

Tear says This one is, I assure you. As is the boat, which will carry us on to Portugal. As are the trains, which will take us to the Netherlands.

I says Then where're we goin?

He says We stay there. In the Netherlands.

I says to him How come, on accounta we got our feet stuck in some wooden fuckin shoes?

Wally says They *do* have wooden shoes. Can't tell who's he sayin that to, or is he just sorta sayin it.

Tear says A few years back, they refused to extradite Wilhelm II to the Allies. If they're not going to give up the exiled Kaiser of Germany, what are the odds they'll send *us* back here, assuming the American cops ever manage to work out where we are?

I turn to Wally and I says You know, Daff did always say she was dyin to go on vacation.

Wally says to me That's true, but…I assume she wanted to come back at some point.

I says You figure she wouldn't wanna go live in the fuckin Neverlands?

Tear says It's a beautiful country, I hear.

Wally says I would just think about it, Sammy.

Tear says We don't have time for that. They'll be checking the cells in just about five hours, and

The front door to Tear's place *swings* open and *slams* against the wall.

I just about jump outta my fuckin pinstripes. Who the fuck enters a goddamned home like that?

Turns out, it's Tear's boys enter a goddamned home

like that. They come in talkin to each other, these four guys here, soundin like somehow every fuckin one of em's havin their own little conversation.

Wally sidles over and looks at the pages on Tear's table. Then he looks at all the guys comin in. So he fuckin sidles up to me and he says The job looks good, for what it's worth.

I ask him You sayin I oughta do it?

He shrugs and says That's up to you. I'm just giving you my professional opinion. The job looks doable.

I says You see on them sheets what's my fuckin purview here?

He shakes his head no.

So I stomp over to Tear and his guys what're all sayin How are ya, and I gotta mention how these guys're all pretty fuckin big. Ain't as big as me, but they ain't exactly gonna have to lean too hard against the wind neither.

I says to Tear then, I says Hey pal, you got big buddies here. The fuck you need me for?

Two of Tear's guys look at me all sunny-eyed, like they can't wait to hear what am I gonna say next. The other two start sizin me up like I'm a pretty lady what smells some kinda rotten.

Tear says to me Strength. There's a portion of this *robbery* – the most important one, in fact, the opening of the vault – that's gonna take some brute force. I'm not so sure the five of us alone could do it. With *you* though…I watched you out in the yard. Christ, you've got some power.

One of the guys sizin me up says to me I heard you

got annoyed a guy wouldn't get off the bench press, so you grabbed the bar, with over 225 on it, and twisted it up like a pretzel.

Another says I heard you tried to dribble a basketball once, and instead of it bouncing back up into your hand, it drove eighteen inches down into the concrete.

A third guy says I heard even those murderers in the mess bring you jars to open, like jars of pickles and stuff.

I hoist a fuckin eyebrow at that, which I gotta figure is further from what's a fuckin possibility than them other two things what'd they just say. I ain't the type lifts weights or bounces balls, but more'n that, I ain't never heard of one grown man handin another grown man a jar for Can you please open this for me. You ever heard of that? I ain't. Either somebody's gotta snatch that jar outta the man's hand, or else the man's gotta slice their palm so bad they bleed out, spendin their final fuckin moments to grab a towel or some shit and keep workin on the jar. And they're givin out glass jars in lockup now? Gimme a fuckin break.

Ain't none of what these three guys said was true, but that jar one's the real howler of the bunch, you ask me.

Still, ain't no percentage in sayin Sorry fellas I ain't as strong as you think, so I says to em Yeah, I ain't gonna turn my fuckin toes in about it, I'm pretty fuckin strong.

Tear says to me So you'll do it.

I says to him How'd you figure that for a fuckin sign-me-up?

Wally says Time's a-tickin, boys.

I says to em Aaaaah. Then I says to em Alright, here's

the deal. I got a *quib quo quo* for ya, or whatever the fuck it is.

One of Tear's guys says *Quid pro quo?*

I says to him Like I said, about whatever the fuck it is.

Another guy says It's Latin.

I says to him Would you give it a rest about it's Latin? Time's a-tickin, like how'd Wally just say it is.

Wally flinched like he wasn't listenin and he says What?

I says to Tear Here's the *quip quap quo.* We do the bank job quick. Splickity fuckin lick. Then you all gotta help me break back into Sing Sing.

They all look at each other, real nervous.

I says to em *And,* I get a cut of the bank haul. *And,* we're sayin that all balances out, far as we done somethin swell for each other. I don't want nobody knockin on my door two years on sayin about I owe you a favor on acc-ounta how ya chipped in on the Sing Sing thing. No debts, no nothin, tonight closes it all out. Got it?

They go back to lookin at each other.

So I says We ain't got time for this shit. I got a buddy's tryin to pull together another crew to do the same thing, minus the bank job. If you're in, I gotta let him know we ain't gonna need their fuckin services. You in?

One of the guys who'd been lookin some kinda charmed to meet me says How are we gonna do that?

I says to him Well, look who ain't likin the shoe's on the other foot, far as knowin the plan. We got a scheme, don't you fuckin sweat about it. Gonna fake a break-out, so's I can break-in.

Tear says We don't have to do that.

I look at him like I'm sayin Would you quit with the fuckin negatations, only I don't say nothin.

He gets my what-do-I-mean and he says There's an easier way. I broke out with the help of someone on the inside. Someone who *works* there, I mean. His shift was up, so he'll be at home. And I know where he lives. He could help get you back in.

I says Fine by me. Alright. We heist the bank, you take me to your guy, I get back in, all in five hours. We can fuckin do it. Right?

Don't nobody say nothin to me.

I says Let's fuckin move!

Everybody starts scramblin. Not all movin in the same direction. Like I just started countin for a hide-and-go-seek, only can't none of them figure where do they wanna crouch behind.

Wally says I'll give them a ring back at my place. Tell Godric not to call Chet.

Tear says I don't have a phone here.

Wally says Oh. I guess I won't do that, then.

I says to Wally Let's just fuckin go back to yours. Makes sense I fuckin leave you there anyhow. On accounta you ain't gonna bring much to a fuckin heist.

He says You are right about that.

One thing Wally is good for though, is makin people do what he wants. Don't take long before he's got everybody out the door in single fuckin file.

2

TEAR'S GUYS ALL TAKE ONE CAR, only Tear rides with us. Feelin like that's on accounta there's some lingerin fuckin distrusts, only I can't tell which direction is that goin in or how bad is it.

Part way through the ride back to Wally's place, Wally's face looks up to his mirror where can I bet he sees Tear in the backseat and says Say, I'm sure the answer's no, but there's no chance your escape might have aroused suspicion amongst prison security, would it? In terms of putting them on a higher alert or anything?

I turn to look at Tear, on accounta that's a good answer and I'm some kinda invested in hearin, er, it's a good *question* is what I meant, and I'm some kinda invested in hearin the *answer,* what better be fuckin good.

Tear don't look the least bit fuckin discommoded about what'd Wally ask. He says No. Mine was an even quieter escape than Samuzzo's. As discreet as you were.

I says to him Who the fuck you callin a discreant?

Wally says Well, that's good. Then he clears his throat. Then he says to Tear Say, do *you* think this is all doable?

Tear says You mean the, uh, everything we have to do tonight?

Wally says Yeah. Drop me off, hit a bank, meet your guy, get back to Sing Sing, stage a break-out, smuggle Sammy back in, all in about…

Tear says We don't have to stage the break-in. We can

talk to my guy, but I don't think we'll need a diversion at all.

Wally shrugs and says Well, five hours, anyway. For whatever we do.

Tear says to Four, if you include transit time.

I just throw my arms up about how come everybody's wantin to shave down the time we got like some kinda fuckin ice statue?

Wally though, he says Right. And I guess I have to teach you to pick a lock in there, Sammy.

Tear says Hm.

Wally and I both shut our traps to hear what's Tear gonna say. I figure that's on accounta both of us are feelin like maybe this ain't so fuckin doable as how doable did we figure it was.

Tear thinks on it and he says We can do it. Yeah. I think we can do it.

Don't neither of us in the front seat pitch a fuckin follow-up, on accounta I figure we both got the feelin that answer's made of fuckin bubbles what'll go *pop* if you even look at em too hard.

3

WE GET BACK TO WALLY'S and open the door and I say Yoo hoo, anybody fuckin home? Then I feel like a fuckin dope on accounta I said Yoo hoo in fronta a bunch of fuckin toughs.

And I ain't just talkin bout the toughs what're Tear's buddies, trailin along behind me. I'm talkin bout the fuckin zoo animals fillin up Wally's pad.

First face I recognize is Thomas, guy I ain't never gonna quit thinkin of as Tommy Toothpick on accounta he's a goddamned pipsquat. Ain't like that was a nickname I gave him on accounta we were fuckin buddies – little bastard tried to kill me once, but hey, who hasn't – but I figure we got to a place was halfway friendly last time I seen him.

Then I spot Chet Crowder. Guy what runs the Paci-FIST meetins. The real ones, I oughta say. I took to runnin fake ones in some of the joints I went to. Just tryin to keep up a fuckin support system, you know what I mean.

I say to Chet Ah shit, too bad you came out all this way, on accounta I don't fuckin need you.

Chet still shows me a tiny fuckin smile. That's the kinda lunk he is, one what's gonna smile at you even after you tell him you ain't got a song in your heart about seein him again.

There's three other fellas with Chet. One's called Louie, I figure I remember him from when did I go to Chet's place. Other two, I ain't never clapped eyes on priorwise.

One of those two fellas I ain't met before, the biggest guy of the bunch, he shouts MOTHERFUCKER!!! and then he throws a chair across the fuckin room. Right at me.

Then lemme tell ya, fuckin *bedlam*.

Wally's shoutin so loud you can't hardly hear the chair splinterin against the wall. There's fuckin stampede noises behind me, then Tear knocks me outta the way and charges at the Paci-FISTers. The fella what yelled first gets low, like he's fixin to use Tear's momentum and toss him out the fuckin window.

So I swing around, grab Tear by the back of his fuckin shirt, and yank him *hard*. Corner of my eye, I see Tear's guys get stuck in the door, all tryin to smush through at once.

With my free hand, I'm pointin at Chet and tellin him Give your guy a time out!

Chet yells the word Gephen! at the guy, which I'da figured for a fuckin telephone company, only from the contexts I gotta figure for this guy's name.

Guy next to Chet, only fucker in the room whose name ain't familiar for me now, he starts bouncin between his feet and sayin Ring of Resolution! Ring of Resolution!

I tell the guy We ain't got time for the fuckin Ring!

Tear's fixin to make another try for Gephen, so I pop him once in the kidney. Medium-soft, nothin too much, just a little hey-how-are-ya.

Tear's guys finally get unstuck from the fuckin doorframe, and come chunderin in with their heads down, leadin with their shoulders like fuckin leatherheads on an easter egg hunt.

Wally's ain't-a-sister appears outta fuckin nowhere, leapin on the table to get eye-level with us bruisers, sockin that fuckin rifle of hers into her shoulder. She says

This isn't a goddamned romper room boys, let's bring it *way* the hell down.

Tear's guys knock into me. I keep a hold on Tear's shoulder and set my feet, tryin to keep from gettin toppled. Only Tear knocks my feet from in front, and his guys are pushin in from behind, so I get fuckin toppled. Tear goes down too, on accounta I got all that weight on his shoulder.

Ends up my jaw *cracks* into the heel of Tear's shoe, what's pointin up now on accounta he fell forward.

I hear Chet yell Let the anger burn through! Don't feed it! It's just a feeling!

Wally's ain't-a-sis…oh, *Ginger,* that's what's she called, she yells I have a gun! Everybody cut it out! I have a gun!

Tear's tryin to get back to his feet. So I start tryin to get back to *my* feet. He gets to his prior to I get to mine. Feet, I'm sayin.

I'm up just enough to see Gephen breakin free of Chet's hold-back, and chargin at fuckin Tear.

Just prior to I'm all the way standin, Tear's guys *thwack* into me from behind again. Only I got my feet some kinda tangled. So I start stumblin forward, further into the fuckin domicile.

Credit where's it fuckin due to Chet, I see all his guys just standin there while Gephen goes to fuckin war against Tear and his guys. Well, they ain't just standin. But they're holdin hands and swayin side to side and shoutin Ring of Resolution! Ring of Resolution! So I figure Chet's lessons about don't be so fuckin violent took or somethin, huh?

Chet's doin his best to pull Gephen back though. His best ain't good enough, but it's swell of him to fuckin try for it. That Gephen guy's just some kinda fuckin huge.

I'm still stumblin here. I ain't got a center of gravity what you'd call quote well-balanced unquote. So I'm travelin, eyes pointin down, flappin my arms like that's gonna do a fuckin thing.

Wally shouts to me Samuzzo! Give us a hand!

I says I'm busy!

Ginger shouts at me Just let yourself fall!

I flap my arms harder and I says to her Not on your fuckin life!

I keep fightin to get my feet under me, especially once Tear and Gephen start goin at it so hard even Tear's guys take a step back, like Jesus, what the fuck. I figure soon as I got my balance back, I'm gonna have to crack their fuckin heads together just to calm em down.

Only problem is, I got my head down, and I'm real fuckin committed to I'm not gonna let myself plop onto the fuckin floor, only I didn't figure for I'm in an environment's gonna share my priorities, cept only in a way what'd I fail to fuckin foresee.

What I'm sayin is, I got my head down so's I don't see the chair what'd somebody knock over til I'm trippin on it.

Then I'm tumblin through the air, and I don't see the window til I'm flyin through it.

Now I'll tell ya, I got a history of fuckin defenestration. You wanna look that word up? Means flyin through fuckin windows. That's a word I know on accounta I done it so many times I one time asked Godric, You got a word for flyin out a window what's got some dignity? That way next time when Daff asks me Jesus Samuzzo, you got a lot of glass in your back or what? Then I can say to her You ain't gonna believe it, but I fuckin defenestrated again. Sounds fuckin classy stead of glassy, get it?

Only thing is, most times I fuckin defenestrate from the first floor. Not like tonight, when am I doin it from floor three. Second time I'm goin out a floor three window in one night, ain't that somethin? It's a load of numbers, anyway. Too bad this time I'm landin on fuckin pavement.

Lucky for me there's a big tree outside what's been hittin the timber gym I figure, got real buff branches what're pretty good for slowin my fall. I mean, they still fuckin hurt, and feels like I thwack down on about a dozen of em, but at least this way I only hit the sidewalk *hard*, as instead of *really fuckin hard*. Still, I feel it bucklin under me. I'm a heavy guy, I already told ya that. I push myself up and look back at the window. On that third story there. I hear all kinds of fuckin screamin goin on, spot some human body shapes writhin around.

You wonderin if it hurt at all, when'd I do a third-floor defenestration and splat down onto the fuckin pavement? You fuckin kiddin me? The hell's wrong with you? Of course it fuckin hurt. I just ain't lookin to go on and on about how much did it fuckin hurt. But it fuckin hurt a *lot*, I'll tell ya.

Limpin back to the front door – and get a load of this,

soon as I step out from under the tree, two of them hunky branches crash down behind me, on accounta I figure I snapped em with my fuckin mass – anyway, I'm limpin on accounta my left leg's feelin some kinda fuckin busted, and I'm just thinkin to myself Fuck, I shoulda launched that fuckin Gephen guy out the window soon as I seen he was trouble. Tear, he's got use to me. He's got a Sing Sing Singsider. Sing, uh…an insider. Gephen? Who the fuck's Gephen supposed to be? Just some fuckin guy ain't got a purpose to serve, cept causin a fuckin ruckus.

Gotta say though, in my fuckin defense, it ain't like I'm a leader of fuckin men here. Naturalwise, I mean. I'm figurin it on the fly. Crash course in the whaddyacallits. You know.

Speakin of interpersonal dynamics: I open the door to Wally's buildin just in time to see Tear and Gephen huggin each other all the way down the stairs, tumblin ass over end. Makin a hell of a racket while they do, swearin and snarlin and smashin holes in the wall with their shoulders, knockin out the banister with their boots.

Now other folks what live in the buildin are pokin their heads out, wonderin what sort of fuckin ark's bein evacuated in their atrium. Wally's yellin at them folks, tellin em Sorry and Don't worry and Go back inside and We're just leaving. He's shoutin up the stairs while Ginger and Godric and the rest of the fuckin Paci-FISTers are galumphin down after the roly-poly muscle tussle.

I step through the door and meet Tear and Gephen

just as they're brawlin to the bottom of the stairs. Just about hidin in a cloud of fuckin dust, they're scrabblin and scratchin so much. I reach in and I grab em both by the first parts of their persons give me fuckin purchase, and I drag em outside. Regularwise that mighta been a feat gives me some fuckin resistance, on accounta these two ain't featherweights, only I got my fuckin mickey up. Fallin out a window's got some seconds to the ground'll do that to ya.

I use my whole fuckin weight for swingin em into the street. Tried to let em go at different times, so's they ain't gonna end up in another pile that's only different for bein over *there*, but they got all kinds of fuckin tangled, so *there* goes the pile.

Smooth as if they ain't just rolled down the stairs and got thrown into the fuckin street, they go back to clobberin on each other, screamin and shoutin but not sayin a goddamned thing.

Windows around us start comin alive. Lights click click clickin on. Half the block's up now, looks like.

Godric pops out the front door and he yells Gentlemen! Let's stop this at once!

Tommy Toothpick ain't but right behind, and he honks about how they don't seem so gentle at present. Does a trick of remindin me how come I ain't taken to Tommy so much, in addition to he took a pass at offin me that one time.

I says to Chet Kinda wild how we all took a pass at offin each other, one point or some otherwise.

He says It's a small community.

I says to him Sure. You wanna gimme a hand on pullin these crocodiles a ways off each other?

He says Sure. Then he nods at his buddy Louie and we all three go in and get to pullin Tear and Gephen a ways off each other.

Louie says to that last guy You wanna help, Robb?

Robb – figurin that's his name – just shrugs, he don't say nothin back.

I grab Tear, give him a big hug right around the fuckin neck, then I walk backwards and he's comin along for the ride. Chet and Louie, they got Gephen pretty well fuckin collared.

Some dope what must figure his door's a lot fuckin tougher to knock off than it is sticks his head out his window and he shouts at us about Shut the fuck up!

Godric hides his face.

Wally shouts back at him Ah, you've snuck a peek at tomorrow night's main event! Will you be coming out to see these two square off in the ring?

Another dope yells You're promoting a goddamned boxing match?! It's after midnight!!

Somebody screams *Horrible* technique!

Ginger shouts Why don't you come on down and show us what good technique looks like, then!

More lights comin on. More windows openin. More fuckin silhouettes.

I says to Tear, real quiet, We'll get him later. But you gotta calm the fuck down.

Tear says Bull*shit.*

I says to him I came to check on your fuckin relations,

didn't I? And that was a fuckin lie what'd you tell me. Outta the two of us, I'm the one's got a fuckin record of straight-shootin.

Tear quits squirmin and turns to look at me. Then he looks over at Gephen and he says to me He killed my best friend.

Turns out Gephen's got fuckin reverse Victrola horns for ears, on accounta he points at Tear and he says That piece of shit killed *my* best friend!

Tear says Payback's a bitch, huh?

Ginger, still holdin a fuckin rifle while she wanders out into the street, she asks Tear If he killed your best friend, why didn't you just kill *him*? What did *his* best friend do?

Tear just folds his arms and he says again about Payback's a bitch, just quieter.

Godric says, in a tone makes clear he ain't never found himself amongst such boisterous fuckin company, he says Well, I suppose you're both even then, yes? So perhaps we can lower the temperature now? And remove ourselves from this *very* public venue?

Everybody keeps makin noises like pasta water on boil.

One of them silhouettes in the windows shouts I'm calling the cops!

Another one yells back I already called em!

First guy shoots back Well I'm already on the phone, so…!

Wally bounces over to me and he says I think you gotta get gone, pal.

Swear to god, I can't figure how can Gephen hear so clear. But he heard that, and he points at Tear and he says You're not going anywhere, asshole! I'm gonna fucking kill you!

Then he tries to make good on his fuckin word by breakin free of Tear's guys. Takes all of em strainin the fuckin veins on their foreheads just to slow him down.

When the noise hittin my ears ain't just shoe leather on concrete, I hear fuckin sirens.

I says to Wally Jesus, we next door to a precinct or what?

Godric slaps me on the shoulder and he says We're lucky if nobody's recognized you yet. But you need to get out of here, *now.*

Tear taps me from the other side and he says We do. Let's go. *Now.*

I take a look down at the fuckin pinstripe prison duds what am I still wearin, and I says to him Fair point. Then I look at Wally, then Gephen, then at all of Tear's guys workin overtime just to hold back Gephen, then back to Wally, and I says to him You're good here?

Wally smiles and says Oh, yeah. I'll make sure we're all gone by the time the cops get here.

I believe him on accounta that's his fuckin speciality. Ain't gonna be the first time he just sorta walked away from a property got too hot for him, neither. You can bet the whole pot he ain't put his real name on the fuckin deed.

He reaches into his pocket and gives me the keys for the car what'd we drive here in.

I says to him Thank, pal. Then I follow Tear off back to where's the fuckin car parked.

4

WE GET TO THE CAR and Tear starts walkin to the passengerside door. Which is to say, we both start walkin to the passengerside door.

I says to him, I ask him What are you doin?

He don't pause til he's got his hand on the handle what pops the door open. *Then* he looks at me and asks me What?

I says to him I sit in the fuckin shotgun seat.

Tear says He gave you the keys. It's your friend's car. I figured

I says to him You leave the figurin to me. I'll do the figurin for the both of us, from there in the fuckin shotgun seat.

Tear frowns at the car door, then up at me. He says I don't know how to drive, man.

I says to him So what?

He just sorta stares at me, til he says Do *you* know how to drive?

I says to him Course I know how to fuckin drive. I just don't care for it, is my position.

Now his eyelids go all heavy. He says to me, real flat-like, he says Well, you think you can hold your nose and get behind the wheel, just this once?

I got plenty I wanna say to that, only more fuckin cop sirens hit my ears, same time as I hear footsteps turnin on to the fuckin block what're we on. People out at this hour, you believe that? Can't be up to no kinda good, lemme tell ya.

Anyway, I make some unhappy barnyard noises and I get behind the fuckin wheel.

I take us back around past Wally's place. Just to see what's the damage. Quit fuckin squirmin about it, I ain't goin *right* past. Just crawlin along at the cross street, like any fuckin lookieloo.

There's seven cop cars out front. Don't see nobody sittin on the curb in cuffs, but still. *Seven.* Fuck.

Tear whistles. Then he says That seems like an overreaction.

I frown. And I says to him, I figure somebody up in one of them windows fuckin made me. Though if that's the what-was-it, seven seems like they ain't sent enough.

Tear makes mumblin noises for a bit. Then he mumbles words, and those words're They could have made me too, and sent the cars for me too. I also broke out of Sing Sing.

I says to him Yeah, but you ain't had your face in the funny pages same way I did.

He goes back to mumblin just noises.

Then we're outta fuckin cross street to look down, and we're just starin at the side of a fuckin brownstone. Yeah, it's that kinda neighborhood. Wally likes the nice stuff.

I drive us on a block, then I says You gotta take me

to your guy, now.

Same time as I'm sayin that, Tear says We've gotta hit that bank, now.

We look at each other like we can't believe what'd the other guy just say.

Tear says The game's up, Samuzzo. You've been spotted outside the prison. Your only shot now is get the money, get out of the country. I swear to you, I'll help get your girlfriend or whoever out after.

I says to him The game ain't even close to up. Only our timeline got fuckin moved. I figure, cops gotta work out which prison am I meant to be in, find somebody's awake at this hour, give em a ring, ask em to check on ol Samuzzo, then they gotta get up outta whatever chair are they sittin in, go *all the way* to my cell in fuckin C Ward, then

Tear interrupts and he says You're making it sound like it's gonna take a lot longer than it will.

I says to him Assumin they even made me, which if they made anybody of the two of us it's for sure gonna be me, but let's how bout we just focus on we got no fuckin idea how long is it gonna take for word gets back. But I'll tell ya, speakin from fuckin experience, the law don't move in straight lines like quite how do they make it out like.

Tear just shrugs and he says They caught us once.

I says to him Yeah, that's my fuckin point. All the crimes I spent my whole life doin, and they only caught me *once* for em? They oughta be blushin pink like prize hogs, they got a record like that.

Tear folds his arms and he says I'm not trying to be a hardass here, but I don't think I've got the same hot streak as you. I've got no interest in skulking around the city as a fucking fugitive. The transport's lined up for tonight, and I need to be on it, or I'm stuck here.

I says to him So you take me to your prison guy, and I'll give you the fuckin car.

He says to me I can't drive, damn you!

I says Oh, so it's my fuckin problem you can't drive?

He says to me Apparently it is now, yes!

I says Seems you're right, turns out!

He shakes his head and looks out the window and says Bussuh sussuh mussuh

I says to him I can't fuckin hear a *word* you're sayin, facin the fuckin window there.

He turns back and he says Besides, I need the money from the bank to pay the ferryman.

I laugh and I says Pay the ferryman.

He asks me Why is that funny?

I quit laughin and I says You know, I couldn't tell ya.

We do a whole block without talkin.

I says You take me to your guy, I'll see Wally helps ya keep your fat head under the fuckin trenchtop. We'll set ya up another

He interrupts me and he says No. No. It's tonight or it's nothing. We do the bank *tonight,* and I help you get

I says I ain't goin to live in a fuckin fairy tale village with ya!

He says Well I'm not taking you to my guy until we've hit the bank!

So I says to him Grrrrr. Then I says Fine. Fine. Where's the fuckin bank?

He says Not far. Just a few block north.

It's only on accounta my heroic fuckin self-control I keep my hands on the wheel, instead of polishin my eyes with my knuckles, so hard it does the *RR-rr-RR-rr* noise. I sputters at Tear, I says to him You wanna rob a bank on *Manhattan?*

Tear thinks on that, then he says I suppose your friend was right, it's more of a heist.

I says You ain't figured one of them ones down in Brooklyn might be easier? Or maybe even Jersey? Assumin they got banks in Jersey, instead of everybody's just stuffin their mattresses?

Tear shakes his head no and then he says No. We know how to hit this one specific bank here. We know how much money to expect. So this is the one we have to do.

I says to him Fine.

And I turn the car fuckin northwards.

That ain't lost on Tear. He sees how many ways can he do a big frown at me, then he says Where are we going?

I says to him North, til you tell me a different which way I oughta go.

He says Why? Only he says it in a way like he knows precisely fuckin why.

I says to him You know precisely fuckin why.

He says We can't hit the bank *right now.*

I says That's too bad, on accounta that's where're we

goin.

Tear turns his fuckin shoulders at me and he says We need to find my boys. This isn't a two-person job! We need...if you can get me to a phone, there are a few safehouse numbers I can

I says I ain't got time for that. Best case, I'm lookin at, I don't know, four hours and some? Not includin the time to...oh, you know, I get why does everybody take that time out now. Anywho, that's best case, but that time-rectangle mighta fuckin shrunk on accounta you and that Gephen guy havin a goddamned wrestle. So you tell me we gotta hit that bank prior to you help me, that suits me like a fuckin haberdasher. We're gonna hit the bank. Just the two of us, right now. I got a plan for poppin the safe cookin already, matter of fact. So what's the bank and where do I turn?

Tear just does swamp noises for a bit, then he says We can't do it with just the two of us. This isn't...this isn't the way.

I says to him I know it ain't the fuckin way, that's how come I'm askin you what's the bank and where do I turn.

He says I've spent ages on this plan, Samuzzo! You can't just blow it up and

I tell him I fuckin said to you about I got a new plan cookin, and if you wanna keep fuckin arguin with me I'll be a gentleman and stop the fuckin car rather than I ask you to tuck and roll while am I holdin speed. We both of us want the other fella's help, but ain't neither of us are likin how're things shakin out. That's called a fuckin compromization. Now what's the fuckin bank, and where the fuck do I turn, or do I gotta stop and ask one of these fuckin nightcrawlers out here?

Tear settles on what's his favorite frown to show me. Then he says Take the next right.

5

HE BANK'S JUST A FUCKIN BUILDIN'S got the word BANK on it. Which, you know, what the fuck. I broke into plenty of buildins, what had plenty of words on em. This one ain't so different, you ask me.

I say as much to Tear and he just shakes his head.

He says Have you ever robbed a bank before?

I tell him Course I ain't fuckin robbed a bank. Way too much heat. Have you?

He says to me Yeah. I got caught. That's why I was in Sing Sing.

So I says Gotta tell ya, that ain't the most optimistical shit what could you have said just now.

Then he gets real serious and he starts explainin all these fuckin security measures what do they got there. They got an alarm what'll start ringin over the door, and more all through the shop too. Telegraph message what'll get sent to a box what'll get checked by some no-bedtime havin kid on watch with fleet feet what'll run to the phone what'll wake up the cops and get em on their way over. Gotta say, Tear knows his shit. He's got this whole fuckin plan for how's he gonna cut this wire and stick cotton in that alarm and on and on and on, and I'm just waitin for him to finish. Like havin Wally here, the way he's runnin his mouth for a marathon rather than a sprint.

Finally he's done, which I know on accounta he says So, I'm *dying* to know, how do you expect us to accomplish all of *that* with only two people?

I point at the bank and I says to him I barely listened to a word you fuckin said, on accounta all I gotta know is how much time is there between I kick that fuckin door in and the cops show up?

Tear just stares at me. He says I told you that information.

So I says And I said to *you* about I wasn't listenin.

He does some more starin, then he says The money's going to be in a vault, Samuzzo. Getting in to the building isn't the challenge. It's getting in to the *vault*.

I shake my head and I says Biggest challenge is doin the whole fuckin heist without we touch anythin. On accounta they can ding you for your fingertip prints you leave behind whenever you touch stuff. You hear about that? That's how'd they get *me,* was the fingertip prints. And the not-so-hostage situation.

Tear says The what?

I says to him Gimme a number. You done all this fuckin library time, I figure you gotta have a number in your head for how many minutes is it gonna take the cops to show.

He says Our plan was to cut the alarms so they *never* show.

I keep on lookin at him.

He says I can give you a number. But do you have a plan?

I just keep on lookin.

He does a kind of shrug makes his shoulders go *down* and he says Playing it safe, assuming they're able to mobilize more or less as soon as they get word, I'd give them eight minutes.

I says to him *Eight minutes?!* How they fuck're they gonna get here in eight fuckin minutes?

Tear says to me I'm erring on the side of caution.

I says to him I'd figure eleven or twelve's more like it.

He says I'm basing my estimate on research. The distance to the nearest station. The chain of communication that'll get word of the alarm to

I says to him Meet me halfway here, let's call it ten.

He says to me This isn't…I'm not the one setting the time here!

I says to him *Nine* minutes.

Tear says *Uuuugh.* Then he turns and looks in the back seat, rummages around a bit, mumblin about Please tell me they put them…

Then he says *Ah* and comes back into the front seat holdin two flops of cotton or some fuckin fabric. I can never remember which fabric goes with which what-does-it-feel-like. They're fuzzy and black, that's all I got for ya.

Tear says to me Put this on, at least. Then he puts his on at least, and turns out they're fuckin full face masks what just leave little holes for the eyes and the mouth.

I look at em, and I says to him Where the fuck you been hidin those?

He says through his little mouth hole at me, he says My bag. Then he hands me some fuckin gloves, which is good thinkin for we ain't lookin to leave the fingertip prints.

I says What bag?

He lifts up a big fuckin bag outta the backseat and he tells me I've had a bag since we left my place. Been carrying it almost the whole time since then.

I says Huh on accounta I ain't noticed the bag. Then I take the mask and while I'm tryin to find the big hole where does my fuckin melon go, I says to him Don't figure this'll do much hidin my who-am-I, on accounta I'm still a fuckin double-wide guy in prison pajamas.

He says It's better than nothing.

I finally get my head through and I says to him You ain't cut fuckin holes in mine!

He says to me You're wearing it backwards.

I crank it around on my head and I'm grumblin bout I put it on just right, you only cut the holes on the wrong fuckin side.

Tear does another big sigh and looks at the bank. Then he says Eight minutes, we're gonna say. You got a plan?

I slide on my gloves and I says to him Yeah. You got a fuckin timepiece?

I was only kiddin, but get this, he goes and pulls a fuckin pocketwatch outta his pocket! Ah, I shoulda told you to *watch,* he pulls the watch...pocket, the whole thing. Missed opportunity for a laugh. Damn.

Anyway, I says to Tear Jesus, your boys did right by ya, speakin of the fuckin sartorials.

He just stares at me.

I says We ready to go?

He says to me I can't believe you know the word *sartorial*.

I says I know plenty of shit. Then I tap the side of my head and I says Library of fuckin Alexanderplatz in here, only everythin but the gift shop's closed for a private event.

Tear keeps on just lookin at me. Then he says I'm struggling to fully interpret what that could mean.

So I says It means *let's fuckin vamoose and rob this bank already, how bout?*

Bout fuckin time, we do that.

6

W **HOLE WAY OVER TO THE BANK,** Tear keeps askin me what's my plan, what's the plan, every variation what can you think of for you're sayin *what* and *plan*. Really just the two what'd I already mention, and then one where you got *our* gettin between them other two words. But he keeps fuckin sayin em so it feels like there's more'n just the three.

Anyway, I don't say nothin til we cross the street and get to the bank, at which fuckin time I flamingo on my foot got it the worst when'd I defenestrate outta that third story window, and use the other to kick in the fuckin door to the bank.

Takes three good wallops, but I get it eventually.

Soon as I knock it in, an alarm starts fuckin trillin. The tinniest, loudest fuckin bell you ever heard, gettin smashed with a little fuckin gong-stick faster'n oughta be allowed.

It says to us *BLBLBLBLBLBLBLBLBLBL!*

Tear clicks a clacker on his clopwatch, and he says to me Eight minutes! Let's go!

I says to him, only I gotta yell it on accounta that fuckin alarm, I yells to him Alright!

The bank's bigger'n how big did I figure it'd be on the outside. Got three windows for the fuckin tellers, and all those got little ledges on em like where's an old lady gonna leave her pie to cool. Across from em are some big fuckin color-glass windows what oughta be in either a church or a fuckin train station, only there ain't no light comin through em so they ain't got the grandeurs what do I figure they oughta.

Alarm's still sayin *BLBLBLBLBLBLBLBLBLBL.*

Tear tells me Seven minutes and forty seconds!

I says to him That's plenty of fuckin time.

I ain't too stressed on accounta we ain't gotta look for the big walk-in safe. A *vault,* I figure that makes it. The massive fuckin circle of a door, with one of them spinny handles in the middle like the wheel of a fuckin pirate ship, it's just sittin out starin at the lobby. Seems like somethin they oughta be hidin, only I figure the place ain't *that* big. And furtherfuckin more, it ain't like folks ain't clued in to they got one of these walk-in lockboxes lyin around.

I point at the big door and I says to Tear Go over there. Could be I'll have some questions for ya!

Tear looks at me like *What the fuck is this guy talkin about, questions,* only I figure he ain't got a better plan, on accounta he does what'd I ask for he does.

Wincin on accounta that *BLBLBLBLBLBLBLBLBLBLBL* is givin me a fuckin headache, I punch through one of the windows of the fuckin teller stall, and climb through over that pie-coolin ledge. So now I'm on the other side like I fuckin work here.

Tear says somethin to me from over by the door. Only I can't hear him.

So I yell to him, I yell Afternoon sir, welcome to the fuckin bank. You want a toaster or some shit?

He yells WHAT THE FUCK ARE YOU DOING?! And that time I fuckin hear him.

I shrug and I says to myself Ain't everybody knows how to have a fuckin laugh. Then I find what am I lookin for here: a telephone.

I pick it up and get the number what do I want in it, then it says to me Ring ring ring til it switches to sayin Debrasco's 24/7 Playing Cards Emporium, how may I help you? in Wally's voice.

I says to Wally Heya pal. What are the odds I knew which fuckin safehouse would you go to next, huh?

He don't say nothin, which I figure is him listenin to the *BLBLBLBLBLBLBLBLBLBLBL* in the background. Then he says to me Well, we went to the closest one, so

I'd say pretty good, as far as those odds you mentioned go. Hey, are you in the middle of doing what I think you're doing?

I says to him Sure am. That's how come I gave you this fuckin ring-a-ding.

He goes back to not sayin nothin.

So I says Remember when you was sayin you could teach me to pick a fuckin lock? You said any lock can be picked, you remember that, that time when'd you say that?

He says Yeah in a way sounds like sandpaper wipin sweat off its forehead.

I says Great. So you gotta talk me through pickin the lock of a fuckin bank vault.

He says Over the phone.

I says to him Yeah. And we got… Then I yell at Tear about How much time we got?

Tear says to me WHAT?!

I tap my fuckin wrist and I says back HOW MUCH TIME?!

Tear looks at his pocketwatch and he says SIX MINUTES AND FIFTY-SEVEN SECONDS!

I says to Wally into the phone then, I says We got seven minutes.

Wally's voice gets real steady, and he says to me What kind of vault is it?

Attaboy. You see how come I got such a big heart for Wally?

I yell to Tear YOU SEE ANY FUCKIN EXPOSITION ON THE VAULT THERE, TELLS YOU

THE WHOLE BRANZINO

WHAT KIND IT IS?

Tear wrinkles his fuckin nose at me, then starts jerkin his head around the whole vault. No sense of fuckin structure to how's he lookin, just swingin his face over every square inch of the thing what can he reach.

Guess what was he doin paid off though, on accounta he calls back to me AMBLY SFV-935… he looks back at whatever is he readin, then he keeps goin with …592-20733!

I says to Wally It's Ambly SFV, then a bucket of numbers.

He says What are the numbers?

I sigh then I make Tear repeat em for me, slow, so's I can say em at Wally one at a time.

At the end of that Tear says SIX MINUTES AND TWELVE SECONDS!

I wave at Tear to ease off with the clock shit, then I says to Wally You feelin like we can crack that?

He says to me I've got a guy I can call, he's a safe guy. As in vaults, er…he can help. If…*yep, I hear ya*…if he can't help, Godric's got a guy too.

I says Godric's there with ya?

Wally says Yep.

I says to Wally Who's got the better guy?

Wally does a fuckin pause, only I figure he's usin it to do some fuckin back-and-forth with Godric. Then he comes back real glum and he says Probably Godric's.

I says Call Godric's guy. Then call me back.

Then I read him the number what's on the phone here. And I says to him Ain't lookin to stick ya too much

125

with the tick-tock, but we're lookin at closer to five minutes now.

He says to me I started a clock too. You're still closer to six minutes than five.

I says to him Not if you keep fuckin runnin your mouth instead of callin Godric's guy, we ain't.

Wally says I'll call ya right back.

I says to him Thanks, pal. Then I hang up.

Alarm's still goin *BLBLBLBLBLBLBLBLBLBL!*

Tear says to me SO WHAT DO WE DO?

I yell to him WALLY'S GONNA CALL GODRIC'S GUY!

I'll tell ya, Tear couldn't look much deeper in the dumps if I'd told him I called the cops myself.

To start with, I ain't too nervous. Bit rattly round the edges, I ain't afraid to say, only I put that down to how loud's the fuckin *BLBLBLBLBLBLBLBLBLBL!* Only I start feelin like I been standin here with my arms crossed, starin at this fuckin phone what ain't ringin, for a while now. I'm startin to worry, is it gonna take this guy so long to tell Wally how do we get into the vault that Wally ain't gonna have time to tell *me,* let alone Tear and I actually do the shit what's he say to do?

I look up at Tear and he ain't even lookin at me anymore. He's pattin his hands all around the fuckin vault door, tryin to turn the big wheel. Like that's all's it gonna take. Silly shit.

Though if this phone don't ring real fuckin soon, I'm the one's gonna be feelin pretty fuckin silly.

I yell at Tear HOW LONG WE GOT?

Tear turns at me, then looks at his watch and yells THREE MINUTES AND FORTY-ONE SECONDS!

Jesus, that makes me flinch. I ain't appreciatin that tone in his voice, like he's the one tellin me bout the time instead of I'm the one asked to hear it, but hey. I can't fuckin blame the guy.

I look back down at the fuckin phone. I'm thinkin *Fuckin Christ Wally, you forget about me or what?*

I look closer at the phone. On accounta it's lookin even more nervy than I'm feelin. Way it's tremblin, I mean.

The fuckin thing's ringin. I only can't hear the fuckin thing ringin over the fuckin alarm!

I pick up the phone and I says to Wally Well?

The phone says to me This is Sergeant McCready with the NYPD, we've received multiple reports that your alarm system has been

I interrupt him and I says Would you get off the fuckin line? I'm waitin on a call.

Then I hang up.

Tear says to me WHAT'D HE SAY?

I shake my head and I says IT WAS JUST THE COPS. FUCKIN IRISH, GOIN BY THE NAME, BUT I AIN'T GOT A PROBLEM WITH THAT!

Tear tells me THREE MINUTES AND TWENTY SECONDS!

I says ALRIGHT ALREADY and look back at the phone. Get my eyeballs right up on the fuckin thing. So close that when it does start ringin, I fuckin goose so hard I pull a muscle in my neck.

So I answer the phone sayin AAAH. Yeah?

Phone says to me I've got a way in.

It's Wally's on the phone, I figure I don't gotta spell out.

I says to him All ears.

He says to me That kind of vault there was made after a bunch of people died in older models made by the same company.

I says to him So what, it's haunted?

He says Not quite, I mean more that people got locked inside the vaults by accident and suffocated and died. The families sued the company, so they installed a bunch of safety measures in these newer models. Very hush-hush, not even in the manuals, particularly the one we're gonna use to get

Tear yells THREE MINUTES!

I says to Tear I'M HEARIN HOW DO WE GET IN, PIPE DOWN! Then to Wally I says Just tell me how do we fuckin get in, I ain't lookin for the historionics.

Wally says to me I don't think you're gonna love your way in, though. So all this background is buttering you up for it, I guess.

I don't say nothin.

He says to me It doesn't involve butter.

Tear shouts TWO MINUTES AND FIFTY SEC-ONDS!

I says to him SHUT UP ABOUT THE TIME! Then to Wally I says Talk faster. On accounta he runs his mouth, but if he's tellin me this is shit I oughta know, I figure I believe him.

Talkin faster now, he says Well, the vault model they've got there has a food tube, so somebody who gets locked inside can still be fed, even if there's nobody around who can open the vault. They're SOL on the restroom stuff, but that's

I says to Wally That somethin I oughta know?

He says to me Nope, sorry about that. Just thought it was interesting. Point is, though, there's also an air vent.

I says We get in through the vent. Great. Where's the fuckin vent?

He says Not quite. The vent's about the size of your… well, of *my* fist. But you see, the last safety measure is the one they didn't put in the manual. The vent and the food tube, which is also about fist-sized, both of which *are* in the manual, they're just behind this access panel so even if they weren't in there then anybody could just flip that little door and see them and be like, what's this?

I says Wally.

Wally says Right, but the very last, when-all-else-fails safety measure is a little dingus that flips when there's too much carbon dioxide in the safe. They don't put it in the manual because that shouldn't ever happen, with all the tubes and vents they have now, and…well, this dingus rather undermines the purpose of a vault. Because if somehow those vents all get blocked up, and somebody gets trapped inside, and they're huffing and puffing away, eventually they'll have huffed up all the oxygen and puffed out enough carbon dioxide to flip this dingus. Next thing you know…and I don't know if it's down to them not imagining a scenario where this could happen in a theft-style context, or if they just felt like it's easier to get taken to court by a bank than a grieving family, or what, but if the dingus flips...the vault unlocks itself. So whoever's trapped inside can get out.

I says to Wally That's some space-age shit.

He says That's what I was thinking, Sammy.

I says So all's we gotta do is get trapped in the vault to open it?

He says No...well, here's the part you're not gonna love.

I says Oh, right. Ain't like I can just *be inside* or what the fuck.

Wally says Exactly. What you've gotta do is flip the dingus, from the outside.

I don't say nothin, on accounta I got no clue how'm I meant to fuckin do that. Til I says to Wally I got no clue how'm meant to fuckin do that.

He says You just have to stuff up the food tube so it's airtight. And you just have to, um, you have to breathe into the air vent. Suck out oxygen, blow in carbon dioxide.

I says to him We got two minutes and change here, where the fuck am I gonna get that much carbon dioxide?

He says That's what you breathe out. Just breathe it into the tube.

I says to him Ain't I gonna run out?

He says Just keep taking in oxygen. Your body will change it over for you.

I says How do I take it in?

He says Breathing.

I says to him Wow, the human body's a hell of a fuckin thing, ain't it?

He says Some are. But I'd work on that vault now if I were you.

I says to him Good thinkin. Thanks, pal.

He says Anytime!

I says to him Alright, bye.

He says to me See ya.

Then I hang up and I go stompin back over to Tear. Somehow I'd tuned out that fuckin *BLBLBLBLBLBL-BLBLBLBL* on the call, only you better believe I'm fuckin hearin it again.

First thing he says to me is One minute and fifty-eight seconds!

I says to him I ain't got time to spin the whole fuckin yarn, you just gotta go with me on this. You got a hankie or some shit?

Matter of fact, Tear's got a fuckin hankie on him.

So I says Hold your fuckin horsies on that.

Then I go lookin for that little door what'd Wally say was the tubes and shit behind. Don't take long to find it, just to the right of the big round door. About the size of a shoebox, this little door is, and I ain't even talkin for shoes what would I wear.

I open it up and feast my fuckin eyes, on accounta it's a tube says FOOD and a vent says AIR.

I says to Tear Gimme the fuckin hankie.

He gives me the fuckin hankie, and I bunch it up and stick it in the tube says FOOD.

The hankie goes slidin right down. Into the vault, I figure.

I says to Tear You ain't stitched your initials or home address or nothin on there, did ya?

Tear says to me What the fuck?

I says to him Alright, we do gotta clog up this fuckin tube, so's we can breathe into the vent says AIR til the vault opens.

Tear just looks at me.

I says to him There's a dingus, on accounta this kinda fuckin vault's a murderer! I ain't got time to lay out the fuckin tapestry!

Tear looks at his watch and he says One minute and

I says to him Quit gogglin your watch and help me clog this tube!

These sloppy fuckin bankers left enough jackets and shit around the shop, it don't take us too long to find enough to clog up the food tube. While we're doin that, Tear puts together how does this fuckin vault work. He says to me There's some sort of carbon dioxide detector in there?

I says to him Yeah.

He says Wow about it. Then after the fuckin food tube's clogged, he says Start blowing. I want to make sure there's no air coming out anywhere else.

I sigh on accounta I was hopin Tear would take the first fuckin at-bat, far as blowin goes, only we ain't got time for I raise a fuckin ruckus about it. So I put my fuckin mouth against the tube says AIR on it, and I start huffin and puffin into it.

Tear's walkin around the fuckin vault, wavin his arms. He says to me I don't feel anything… Then he looks over at me and he says No, Samuzzo, you're just blowing *at* the tube.

I says to him I'm blowin in the fuckin tube! That's what'd Wally tell me I gotta do!

He says You're just blowing *at* it! You need to get your lips around the vent, to create a seal so

I says to him I ain't fond of havin a grown man tell me what oughta I do with my lips.

He says What, should I go find a *kid* to talk you through it? Because we

I says I ain't happy *anybody's* talkin to me about what're my fuckin lips doin!

He says to me Forty seconds, Samuzzo! Get your lips around it!

So alright, I fuckin do that. I ain't lookin to dwell on the fuckin experience, but I huff and puff down the fuckin vent. Then Tear comes in and he does it for a bit. We take fuckin turns gettin our lips around it, tryin to cover the vent with our fuckin hands when're we movin our faces off it. Gettin real quick looks at each other's eyeballs, lookin like This shit *stays between us,* til the day do we fuckin die, and even then.

Certain point, while I'm on the huff-n-puff, Tear looks at his watch and he says Uh oh.

I make a noise like *What* while am I still on the huff-n-puff.

Tear says to me We're past zero.

I look at him and I says On the

He shouts Cover the vent!

I cover the fuckin vent and I says to him On the countdown?

He says Yeah.

I give him a real hard squint and I says So that whole eight minutes you were so fuckin in love with, you just yanked that outta your recesses, huh?

He says I told you, it was a conservative estimate based on thorough research.

I says to him You ain't researched the fuckin vault, can't help but notice.

He says We had an entirely different way to crack it! One we needed the *whole team* to accomplish!

I shake my head and as I'm puttin my lips back on the vent I'm mumblin Well now we don't know when're the cops gonna fuckin show.

I huff and I puff and I figure I blow the fuckin vault open, on accounta the door yells *CLICK*.

Tear and me, we just stare at each other. Mouths hangin open, with our chapped fuckin lips.

Christ, lemme tell ya, I ain't hardly ever moved so fast in my fuckin life.

7

MASTER OF FUCKIN PLANS OVER HERE, Tear I'm talkin about, he ain't thought about how ain't neither of us got sacks to load up til we're in the vault. Left his precious fuckin bag in the car, even. The alarm's still screamin though, and the cops're gonna bust in any minute, so we just start grabbin all the shit what's loose. Tear figures that ain't gonna work for him, so he runs out and finds they got fuckin duffels behind the pie-coolin counter. While he was off gettin those, I had a go at rippin out some of the fuckin safe deposit boxes. And I ain't tryin to be a fuckin boastard bout how strong am I, but turns out it's real easy. I just pop the boxes half-strength, like I wanna break their nose without sendin it through the far side of their head, and they come right on out. So I start stackin those up.

Little over a minute goes by, and we're back in the car, on our fuckin way.

Not a block out from the bank, we see cops runnin their lights, haulin ass for where'd we just fuckin come from. Tear starts slappin the dash and makin Yahoo and Yippee noises.

I'm some kinda fuckin delighted right alongside him, only my ears're still ringin from the fuckin alarm. So I says to him Alright there buddy, let's dial down, huh?

Tear dials down a bit, only he's still fuckin trillin like a songbird. He spins around in his seat and beholds our fuckin loot and he says That's my freedom! I'm *free!* I can finally get out of this fucking country!

I says to him What, you don't like this country?

He says Of course not! Do you?

I says Not since they started bein able to ding ya by your fingertip prints, I guess not. Up til then I ain't had no foul fuckin feelins though.

He shakes his head and he says This country, oh…ah, I don't want to get off on it.

I says You better not. You get off on your time, pal.

He looks at his precious fuckin pocketwatch, and he says Alright, I've gotta make my pickup, so let's get you connected with Howard quick.

I says to him Who the fuck's Howard?

He says My

I interrupt him and I says Right, your guy from the prison, let's go pay Howard a fuckin howareya.

So we do that. Drive on out to Howard's place, in a pretty shitty spot some ways north of the city. In the direction of fuckin Sing Sing, which I'm feelin sunny we're movin that way.

We pull up outside Howard's pretty shitty house, then Tear says to me So…he's not gonna be too happy to see me. He'll be even *less* happy if it's more than me that he's seeing. So you wait here, I'll wave you in if he's on board.

I remind Tear It ain't really an option, does he wanna be on board or not.

Tear nods and says If he's not on board, I won't have to wave you in. You'll know when to come.

Then he gets out of the car and starts walkin up to the house. And it is a house, ain't a fuckin apartment complex. Shithole though, like I mentioned. I gotta figure they ain't payin these guys a princely fuckin sum.

That's a surmise gets fuckin confirmed when Tear comes back quick and pops in the back seat to grab a handful of the loose fuckin banknotes. Kinda surprised Howard trusted a fuckin con enough to get paid on the back end, only maybe there was some up-front I ain't privy to. Either way, I don't say nothin on accounta both me and Tear are on a fuckin clock.

Speakin of, prior to he's done grabbin the cash I says to Tear How much time til they're countin heads up in the hoosegow, you figure?

He takes another peek at his pocketwatch and he says to me Three hours, give or take.

I just nod and settle back in my fuckin seat on accounta what else am I gonna do?

Tear's got whatever's he gonna give Howard, so he climbs outta the backseat and slams shut the door and heads back on up to the shitty house. Bein *real* fuckin suspect, lookin this way and that before knockin on the door. Don't nobody answer, so he knocks again. Lookin both ways again.

I says to myself in the car, I says Easy does it, pal. Only Tear obviously ain't in a spot where can he hear me, so it feels like I'm sayin to myself bout easy does it. Which, funny enough, kinda makes me feel more at my easy. Even though I got that fuckin clock tockin' down, one tick at a time.

The door cracks open a bit on the house. So Howard's home. Don't look like he's welcomin Tear in, though. He's talkin to him through the fuckin doorcrack. I can see Tear's shoulders gettin tense. Hope he can easy does it there.

I take a look in the backseat, and all the shit what'd we pull outta the safe. And I just now put together…I ain't gonna get a cut of this. Near to a positive, that ain't happenin. On accounta Tear's gettin on a boat to the fuckin Netherworlds tonight, and what, he's gonna stop off and bury some loot for me, then send me a goddamned map's got a big X what marks the spot? No. Just on the logisticals, there ain't time to organize a how's-he-gonna-get-me-mine. But fine, you know? This ain't gonna be the last score what am I ever gonna be part of. Point is, this is the means to my fuckin end of not bein a lam guy, a guy on the lam. And anyway, Tear's a swell fella. If somebody's gotta take my cut, I'm some kinda chirpy bout it's him.

Still…gotta be a whole load of fuckin dollars here, once you fence the stuff ain't tender on its own. Just think of all the fuckin whole branzinos I coulda bought with all that fuckin money. Oh well. But also *fuck me,* you know? Both of them things at once.

Hell of a night this turned out to be.

I look over towards the shitty house and see the front door swingin open, and Tear followin his kickin foot inside. Rollin his shoulders, bunchin his fist, makin himself look even bigger'n he is.

Like he's about to beat the hell outta whoever's in there.

So I figure Howard wasn't on board.

I get outta the car, but I don't hustle quite the same way as how'd I do in the vault.

THE WHOLE BRANZINO

8

THE DOOR'S ONLY ABOUT HALF on its fuckin hinges when do I walk through it. Boy, Tear's got a hell of a leg on him, how about that?

Anyways, soon as I step on through, somethin fragile hits my face and goes *crack*. It ain't like it hurt all that bad, and you better believe it ain't the first fuckin pottery what'd I break with my face, but I still says to the world The fuck?! I maintain my fuckin locomotion and trip over a lampshade, which is how do I know it was a lamp clonked me on the noggin.

Little guy what's gotta be Howard is jukin from the far side of a table, tryin to keep it between him and Tear, throwin whatever he can get his grubby little mitts on in the meanwhile. I know, it ain't fair I'm bargin in to his home and castin fuckin aspersions on how clean are his hands, but in my defense, the son of a bitch just clonked me on the noggin with a fuckin lamp's meant for readin a goddamned book.

So I says to Tear What the fuck's goin on?

Tear says to me I've got it under control!

I says to him Yeah, I was only just thinkin to myself about how under control is this fuckin tableau.

The little guy yells at me Help! Then he gets a good look at me and he pauses and he says Hey, aren't you

Then Tear leaps clean over the table and you ever seen a snake goin after a mouse? One time I knew this guy

139

called, well, he figured it'd be real hip if he got himself
called Scales, he wanted that to be his *thing*, so he bought
a fuckin snake and he'd feed it live mices, then ring up
his chums, invite em over and say to em Get a load of
this. Then he'd throw one of the mices in, and you'd
figure the snake ain't had a square meal all fuckin year.
The hell ever happened to Scales, anyway? The guy. Ain't
heard from him. Oh, wait. I figure he was the guy had
the thing with the…oh, yeah. Poor Scales.

Anyway, that ain't the thing. The thing's Tear pouncin
on this little guy like Scales' snake on a mice.

Howard's just got time enough to say Uh oh. Uh oh.

I move round the table quick as seems casual and I
says to Tear Maybe go on easy on the little guy, less he
done somethin real rotten, in whichwise then lemme at
him!

Tear don't seem like he's puttin much muscle into the
arm he's got round Howard's neck, on accounta the
arm's already got all the muscle it needs.

I says to him Ain't he helped you escape?

Tear says to me You know he did.

So I says You got a funny spin on gratitude.

Little guy says Aaaach aaaaaach aaaaaaaaaach. He's
slappin Tear's arm, only Tear ain't lookin like it's bother-
in him none.

I says I think you're flippin his fuckin carbon dioxide
dingus, metaphoricalwise.

Tear says I'm just letting him know, it's in his best
interest to help us out here.

I shrug and says Just don't hug him so hard he turns

into a fuckin vegetable.

Tear says I know what I'm doing.

Howard says Aaaaach aaaaaach aaaaach.

Tear keeps squeezin til the little guy's face goes a red onion color, then he lays off.

Straight away, Howard's gaspin and gawpin, rollin around the floor. Tear pushes up to his feet, then looks down at the guy like he feels bad for him, like he just come upon the poor guy like this.

When it's a whole minute's passed and Howard's still rollin around, I says to Tear You figure you mighta maybe been a bit too fuckin persuasive about he's gotta help us?

Tear just shrugs.

I crouch down and I grab the little guy by the shoulders, and I says to him Howar-ya, Howie?

I don't know does he get my joke on his name, on accounta when you just say it it don't sound like a joke. But once I got hands on him in a way ain't lookin to squeeze him into a vegetable, he takes a deep breath and gets some kinda verbal. He says to me Howard.

I ask him You ain't got a funny nickname might get us half way towards bein pals?

He shakes his head No.

So I says You ain't a Howie?

He just shakes his head again.

So I smile at Tear and says Hey.

Tear don't know me so well, so he just says Yeah?

I says to him Howie know if he's tellin the truth?

Tear frowns and says We're losing time.

I says to him Well shit, you were the one givin him a hug what'd take up a whole reel of motion picture footage, but I can't have a fuckin laugh?

Tear don't acknowledge what'd I say. He leans over Howie and he says Samuzzo broke out tonight, but he shouldn't have. You're going to help us get him back in. Right now.

Howie says I can't. I'm already

So I interrupt him and I says You know what you got Howie, is a fuckin defeatist's attitude. You know what happens to folks got defeatist's attitudes?

He says Gulp.

I says to him Nothin. On accounta what are they gonna do but sit at the fuckin speakeasy and run up a tab they ain't never gonna pay off. Fellas what get ahead, they're the one's got the fuckin sunshine disquisition. Us, as a for instance. Tear and me, we got a fatal case of the fuckin optimisms. That's how come I trust you wanna help me out. On accounta I got a nose for folks got good stuff in their heart. Like you. You got a heart's got good stuff in it, Howie. I smelled it from across your fuckin threshold.

He lifts up his chin at me and he says My *name* is *Howard.*

I says to him See, look at that fuckin courage you got. Like one of them brave fuckin sword robots from ye olde legends.

Howie stares at me like he ain't heard of the sword robots.

Tear says to me Are you thinking of…knights?

I says I don't get what does that question mean.

Howie says Those were humans wearing armor. Not robots.

I interrupt him and I says Would you give it a rest about the time of fuckin legends already? I'm sayin you got a big heart, so you're gonna help me out.

So he says Gulp again.

Tear crouches next to me. I figure he figured I was pausin on accounta I'm passin some sorta baton. I figure that on accounta Tear says You wouldn't want to try to prove my friend wrong, Howard. Otherwise he might have to take your heart out, open it up, see first-hand if he was wrong or not.

Howie looks at me. I just shrug on accounta maybe that ain't the way I was figurin to handle it, but long as it gets fuckin handled, know what I mean?

So he tells his neck take a load off, and plops his head back on the ground. Then he goes Huuuuuuuh.

I says to Tear I figure that's the sound of a fella bein fuckin persuaded.

Howie don't lift up his head, so he's mostwise talkin to the ceilin when he says I can get you inside the prison. But I can't help you past that. I don't have the keys to the cells.

So I says Hey, that's fuckin swell of ya.

Now he lifts his head at us, me and Tear, and he asks So you're both going back in?

I says to him Just me.

He nods and he says to just me, some kinda confident all of a sudden, Okay. So it's *you* who'll be owing me a favor.

I nod at Tear and I says to Howie You want my buddy here gives ya another hug?

Only Tear says Hey, I had to do him a favor to get out. Only fair you have to do one to get in.

I asks Tear What was your fuckin favor?

Tear just looks at the bridge of his nose and he says to me *Who*. And nobody you know.

I boggle my fuckin eyes at Tear and I says to him In the big house?

Tear nods at me.

I says Was it that guy what'd we all think hung himself some weeks back?

Tear shrugs in a way tells me that's just who was it what'd he off.

I look at Howie and I says to him Look at you, callin in fuckin hits.

He smiles at me.

I says to him Alright. While we're all just fuckin talkin here, who you want I would off for ya, so's you lend me a fuckin hand on the break-in?

Howie smiles a bit fuckin bigger.

Then he points at Tear.

I frown and follow his finger.

Tear's still lookin at his nose or some shit. He ain't figured what's goin on. That Howie just asked me to fuckin kill him.

Which means I got a single fuckin second of a jump on Tear.

So I jump.

9

FASTER THAN ANYBODY'S got fuckin reactions, I shoot my hand out. And I grab that pointin fuckin finger what's Howie usin to tell me I oughta kill Tear.

I turn it like a fuckin doorknob. Howar-ya, come on in. Now the nail on his pointer's lookin at the ground, even while the rest of em are lookin at the ceilin.

Howie says Aaaaaaaaach again, like he's tryin to make it a fuckin catchphrase.

Ain't til I got the finger turned wrong way round that Tear quits studyin his own fuckin schnoz and checks in with what's goin on in front of him.

I says to Howie Here's the fuckin problem for ya, is I figured you for a fella's got a good heart. So as a fuckin consequence, I figured you for some kinda fuckin pal.

I lean on his finger a bit, on accounta I'm worried if I twist it more is it gonna tear like a sausage off a fuckin link or what.

Then I says Thing about bein pals is, ya do right by each other just on accounta bein pals. If ya only wanna do somethin on accounta you figure there's a different somethin comin your way outta that somethin you done, that ain't bein pals. That's bein partners. Which ain't the same as bein pals. And lemme tell ya Howie, I never fuckin met you before. So we sure as hell ain't partners. I figured us for pals, though. You tellin me I figured wrong?

Howie says Aaaaaaaach aaaaaaach aaaaaaaach in a way seems fuckin agreeable.

So I turn his finger back the way's it meant to go.

He pulls his hand into his chest and makes boo hoo noises. He asks me Is that how you treat your friends, then?

I says to him Only when I wonder if they maybe ain't my friends after all.

He says to me So you have to bully people into being your friend?

I says Nope. I just sometimes gotta remind em what're the perks.

Tear puts a hand on my shoulder. First I figure he's tellin me calm down, which don't make a lick of fuckin logic to me, only then I figure he's doin it as a pal. On accounta I didn't try to fuckin kill him when'd I have the chance, I figure.

So I says to Howie How bout we give this another shot, eh Howie? You wanna help me get back into Sing Sing or what?

Howie growls at his hand like it went and twisted itself. Then he looks at Tear and he says You're not gonna back me up on him having to do me a favor?

Tear says Obviously not, you piece of shit! No!

Howie says I made *you* do me a favor! If *he* doesn't have to do a favor, then you basically look like a chump, doing favors for no

Tear interrupts him and he says Your favor for him was to *kill me!*

So Howie says You were trying to kill *me!*

Tear says to him No I wasn't, I was just trying to choke you a little!

Howie says I didn't think he'd actually *do it*, anyway! I was kidding around!

I says to em Alright, now it's my turn I tap my fuckin wrist. I got…what do I got, two and a half hours to be haulin ass up to Sing Sing? And that's only if I wanna be cuttin it so close it melts in fuckin butter before you even got the heat on.

Howie says What the hell do you want back in for, anyway?

I says to him Long fuckin story, but the headline's bout how I gotta get back in before they do the fuckin who-do-we-got or else I'm livin out my days on the lam.

Howie says You see if I give a toot!

I says to him You *asked* me, Howie. I was only answerin your fuckin question what'd give me the figure about you givin a toot.

Tear says to him How about I *make* you give a toot, Howard, and then some?!

Howie looks from me to Tear, back and forth, over and over. All squirrely.

So I sigh and I says to him Here's your favor Howie, how bout I give you ten thousand dollars?

That straightens Howie's eyebrows out alright. He looks at Tear. Then back at me. Slower this time. Then he says to me You have that kind of money?

I says to him Course I fuckin do.

Tear looks some kinda antsy, and he says to me That's

not coming out of…?

I says to him No. Then to Howie I says You tell me we're on for this, I call my pal Wally, set up a drop. Money won't come to ya til and fuckin unless you get me back in the big house. Just in case you figure for wantin to do any kiddin around like about how I oughta kill Tear.

Howie's mouth pops open and I know what the fuck he's gonna say, so I says to him I know you ain't guaranteein you get me back in the cell. Through the door's good enough.

He lowers his nose and wriggles it around a bit. Then he says Alright. Ten thousand dollars. It's a deal.

I says to him What a fuckin pal you are.

Howie nods, then he looks at Tear outta the side of his eye and he says You think he'll fit?

Tear says I wouldn't have brought him here if I didn't.

I says to em Fit where?

Howie looks kinda startled at me and he nods at Tear and says He didn't tell you?

I says No he ain't told me, what ain't he told me?

Howie asks me Are you claustrophobic?

I says to him Course not. Everythin's a tight fuckin space to me.

So he asks me Do you have any allergies?

I says to him You gotta start puttin some fuckin detail on this, Howie boy. You hidin me in a fuckin coffin or what?

Tear laughs.

Howie's fightin a giggle down too. He says to me It's *Howard.* And not quite.

MISE EN PLACE:
GEPHEN

THE WHOLE BRANZINO

GEPHEN SEMPLE BLAMED PROHIBITION. It wasn't as though he had some elaborate causal framework charted out; the timing just worked. See, round about when the Eighteenth Amendment was being scribbled into law, nearly every bruiser Gephen knew took ill with a dangerous, contagious affliction: sentiment. Some of it, he had to concede, was probably due more to the lately-concluded war than top-down tee-totaling, though the latter certainly couldn't have helped. Plenty of toughs had happily clambered onto the first Europe-bound steamer they could find, their reasoning having less to do with patriotism than with pure machismo. After all, almost all of them had been dandled on the knee of some relative who'd taken up arms against his brother in the Civil War, or else raised in their long, gloomy shadow. So across the sea those tough guys went, where they encountered a war that couldn't have been much more starkly different from the one their grandfathers had fought in if it had been waged via a series of competitive eating contests. Alas, they were the ones getting chewed up: the so-called Great War was a meat grinder, and those who survived returned home with important bits shaved off.

Seemed something close to sadism, far as Gephen was concerned, for cowardly politicians to see such men returning home and think *uh oh, better hide the booze*. Had drowning their sorrows been an option for the returning toughs, perhaps the rot of introspection could have been contained before it spread.

Instead, the world got people like Chet Crowder.

Gephen had, despite listening to the guy talk *quite a lot* about himself, come to learn very little about Chet, biographically speaking. The *de facto* head of Paci-FIST mostly prattled on about contemporary concerns, fears, *feelings*. No matter how firmly toned his musculature may have been, Chet Crowder was a deeply, fundamentally *squishy* man, a quality that struck Gephen as nearly profane. It wasn't that he didn't like Chet, or any of the other bruisers that man had browbeaten into gathering in various sitting rooms around the tri-state area and bellyaching on a semi-regular basis. They all, or mostly, seemed like fairly decent guys. No, it was that they *offended* Gephen. Their mewling seemed a betrayal of their physiques. It seemed a mockery of their professional ethic. It seemed, at bottom, a *personal affront* to Gephen's sense of self-sufficiency. Look at how the British had comported themselves during the war, with their stiff upper lips and general sense of studied condescension! How could any hot-blooded American live with himself, allowing those crown-kissing dandies to best them in the art of composure?

A pressing question, Gephen felt, yet not one it seemed prudent to pose just now. Not from here in the middle of an impromptu Ring of Resolution, held in the gloom of a lightly-trafficked sidestreet in Harlem.

No matter what he said in these fucking things, it only seemed to encourage the Paci-FISTers.

"I understand you're hesitant," Chet cooed, "but your reaction to seeing Samuzzo's friend was anything but."

Louie and Thomas nodded and made *mhm* noises.

"I'm not *hesitant*," Gephen snapped. "I don't have anything to say about it."

"And yet," Thomas noted, "you just told us that you *weren't going to forget that motherfucker a second time.*"

"You did say that," Chet noted.

Gephen rolled his eyes. God. Why did he, one of the most feared and respected enforcers in the business, stand there and take it? When he'd first learned of Paci-FIST, he'd attended out of sheer incredulity. Surely such a limp-wristed gaggle of mercenaries couldn't possibly exist, could it? Turned out it *could*, and before his first meeting was up, Gephen knew he would be coming back. His purpose in doing so was not to unburden himself, but to unburden the others. Steer them away from this navel-gazing madness, bring them back to the rational world. The one where if you weren't bleeding, you were fine.

The only person he'd managed to convince of this truth was Robb, who was now nodding and making his own *mhm* noise.

It had long since become apparent to Gephen that any hopes of making further converts were vain. And yet, he still came to the meetings. Every single one. Why?

He couldn't begin to imagine. Until tonight. For now, there suddenly seemed a wonderful purpose to all the time he'd wasted listening to grown men weep into each other's shoulders. Providence had reunited him with Tear, a bastard about whom he'd completely forgotten.

Yes, Providence. Gephen wasn't a particularly religious fella, but he'd been raised with a lenient enough brand of Catholicism that he'd never felt the need to formally lapse. As a result, it didn't strike him as particularly implausible that this could be some sort of heavenly ledger-balancing. He'd waited patiently, listened as these gooey goons griped about their livelihoods, even gone through the motions of consoling some of them. He'd volunteered for this wacky adventure of helping Samuzzo because he'd thought he might be able to use it to shepherd some of the Paci-FISTers free from Chet's flock, and with a minimum of hand-wringing (or, at least, ensuring somebody's neck was between those hands before they got going). Now, though? He knew what it was all about. Had *always* been about, in a way.

Tear. He could kill Tear, and justify all of this tedium, all of this inaction, all of those moments when he felt *himself* going a bit mushy...which simply wouldn't do.

The mushification. No. No.

No.

"What the fuck are we doing?" he demanded.

Robb agreed with a few more *mhm* noises, each time experimenting with the punctuation he slapped on the end.

"We're helping you understand your aggression," Louie replied, shooting a *how'd-I-do* look to Chet.

Chet smiled and nodded.

Louie beamed.

Gephen rolled his eyes. "I understand my aggression perfectly. Tear killed my best friend. So I'm fucking gonna kill Tear."

Thomas flounced nearer to Gephen and tried to put a hand on his shoulder. Gephen hooked his own arm up and slapped away Thomas' attempted affections.

"Revenge won't bring your friend back," Thomas practically whispered.

Another good eye-roll was in order. "Oh, you're *kidding*. I thought it would."

"Sarcasm is a shrinking refuge," Chet belched with monstrous self-satisfaction.

The other Paci-FISTers whinnied something similar. Even Robb. Gephen shot him a sharp look, which seemed to slide right between the ribs. Good.

"So what are we doing, then?" Gephen demanded. "We're just standing around like a bunch of assholes, talking about how *absolutely crazy* it is that I want to kill the guy who killed my best friend?"

"Nobody said crazy," Louie ventured. He looked to

Chet, then once more embarrassed himself with a child-ish smile.

"He killed your best friend," Chet reminded Gephen, "because you killed *his* best friend."

Gephen actually scoffed. Another one of those things he'd picked up from the English. "So that makes it *okay?!*"

"Of course not. But it means you'd be perpetuating a cycle of violence." Chet drew closer, breaking the circle to cross it and approach Gephen. "You have the chance to close it out. You can make the choice to not be defined by an outmoded sense of honor or retributive justice."

Robb raised his hand. "Can I say something?"

"You don't need to ask *his* permission," Gephen spat. "..."

"You don't need *anyone*'s permission," Thomas explained gently.

"Oh." Robb blinked at this new information. "Thanks. Uh. Well," and then he turned to Gephen.

Oh boy.

"When you refer to the dead guy as your *best friend*," Robb confessed, "it makes me feel kind of, um, sad? Because I do think of you as *my* best friend, and I really thought we were best friends together, with each other. So, uh, if the dead guy is still your best friend, um, I'm just wondering, what am I?"

Gephen could only blink at his lone apostle, who, it appeared, had felt the need to lapse. Formally.

"What are you thinking about?" Chet prompted

Gephen.

Gephen scratched the stubble on his chin. "I, uh…I didn't realize…that's, I mean, that's very flattering. That you think of me like that. I guess for *me*, I just…" he blinked, then flailed his arms as though battling a swarm of bees. "No! Nope!"

"You were so close," Thomas encouraged him.

"Fuck no. Fucking get out of my face with that shit."

"You're using profanity as a shield," Chet observed, like a big old bitch.

"Oh, what? I never heard you say that to Samuzzo, and he swears fucking a hundred times more than me!"

"Yeah," Louie allowed, "but he's better at it than you."

Robb collapsed deeper into his shoulders. "I just want to know what I am to you."

Gephen felt his eyes blinking out of sync with one another. "You're just a friend!"

"Just?"

"Not *just*. But not, obviously you're…you're a *good friend!*"

"But I wanna be your *best* friend!"

"Best friends are for children!"

"You said the guy Tear killed was your *best* friend!"

"Well I'm not gonna be best friends with a fucking fairy who just wants to sit on a pickle and talk about his *feelings!*"

One would expect, given the nature of sound waves and linear time, that the word *feelings* would be the one to echo down the empty street, racing west and east to share what Gephen couldn't. Inexplicably, perhaps by another sort of divine intervention, the word that echoed was in fact *pickle (ickle ickle ickle)*.

The five men in the street paused for a moment of shared recognition that, boy, you really wouldn't have expected *pickle* to be the word that got traction re: refraction.

Gephen folded his arms and declared "I'm done with this shit. Are we done? I'm done. D'Amato's off somewhere else, finding another way into the prison. With Tear. So this little Paci-FIST fucking playdate is over."

Which gave Tear an idea. Hearing himself speak, he inspired himself. Which made him wonder why he ever felt like he'd needed other bruisers by his side.

"Not great at swearing," Thomas muttered under his breath.

Gephen only *just* managed to avoid stomping his foot. "Oh, *fucking* you guys! Enjoy your goddamned pickles, I'm gonna go do something with my fucking night, thank you fucking *very* much!" Gephen turned and followed the echoing *ickle ickle ickle*s out onto the avenue.

Yeah, fuck those guys. Forget em. Fuck em and forget em.

Not like Tear, though. Tear was a dead man. Gephen wasn't going to forget him a second time. Oh, no. He wasn't going to let him get away next time.

Next time as in, later tonight. Where Gephen knew he could intercept him: on the road to Sing Sing.

STEP THREE:
CUT CAVITIES AND SEASON

THE WHOLE BRANZINO

1

I **SAYS TO HIM** Ain't no fuckin way.

Ain't no fuckin way on accounta first off, it's too fuckin small. Might be I'm gonna fit if I can figure out how do I retract my arms and legs like a fuckin turtle, but that ain't gonna help I'm lumpy. Sure, my lumps're muscle, but when ya get down to it, lumps is lumps. And I got em.

The lumps is second so now we're talkin third off, how'm I gonna breathe?

Fourth off, the story don't make no sense.

I relay this shit to Howie and Tear, and they say to me Don't worry about that.

I says to em Don't worry about fuckin breathin?

Tear shakes his head and says Just don't get any of the stuffing in your mouth or nose, and you're fine.

So I says Well what if I do? On accident?

He says I guess you wouldn't be fine, then.

Howie stands up from shovin tufts of stuffin into the empty mattress and he says I don't know what you're complaining about. You've got the easy job. Once we sew you in, all you have to do is hold still and keep quiet. I'm the one who has to move you. By *myself,* since this asshole can't hold his vacation off long enough to help.

When he says that last thing he points at Tear.

I says to Howie He's done his fuckin part here. Don't you go draggin him.

Howie don't respond to what'd I say, he just gets back to shovin in the stuffin, and he says *And*, I would add, I have to move the you-filled mattress in a way that makes it look like it doesn't suddenly weigh almost three hundred pounds.

Tear says to me I'll be honest with you, holding still and keeping quiet's not as easy as it sounds, when you're getting knocked around so much.

Howie turns on Tear and he says That sounds like a comment.

Tear shrugs and he says You had to make it look good, I get it.

Howie says to Tear I *said* I was sorry.

Tear says to him I didn't hear that the first time.

So I says Maybe on accounta you had fuckin stuffin in your ears. Then I turn to Howie and get this, I says to him And maybe you got it in your fuckin *brain,* on accounta how's it gonna make sense you took a mattress outta lockup when you're clockin out, and just a few hours later you're bringin it back when it ain't even back to your fuckin shift yet? The fuck you tell em so'd they let you take the mattress *out*, anyway?

Howie says I just told them I needed a mattress. I told them my wife threw me out, and there was an extra mattress in storage, and so I asked if I could take it to my new place. They said yes.

Tear makes a show of lookin around the joint and he says Safe to assume the wife story was a lie.

Howie shrugs and he says I mean, I didn't specify *when* it happened. And shouldn't you be on a boat to wherever you're going?

I ask him They let you take a fuckin mattress? Just like that?

He says It's not like I ran it up the chain of command. Hey Warden, can I take a mattress? Obviously not. I asked the people who could stop me on the way out the door, and only them. Then he scratches his arm and he says Lot more goes out the door than you'd think.

I says to him The windows, too!

Howie thinks on that for a second and he stands back up and he says Yeah. But look, I get what you're...what all these questions are about. It's gonna be suspicious, me rolling right back in with the mattress. But it's not like I can park outside and do a lap going, oh, hey, anybody gonna have a problem with me showing up off-hours and bringing back the mattress I just left with? That's only going to make it *more* suspicious. We just have to go for it.

I walk up to the mattress and grab a fistful of the fuckin stuffin off the floor, and have a good old fuckin gander at it. Wonderin to myself, how come it's fuckin wet? Only thinkin on how this is the stuffin what'd Tear get packed into this with, maybe I ain't lookin to probe that fuckin what-is-it too hard.

Then I stick my head in, just for a quick look-see on how's it gonna feel when am I stitched up in the fuckin thing. Hot as fuckin stage fright in there, and lemme tell ya, it don't smell much better.

Howie says to me I'm confident I can get you to storage. I am…reasonably confident. But from there, you're on your own.

I says Yeah. I fuckin know about I'm on my own.

I can hear Tear fiddlin with his precious fuckin pocketwatch, then he says On that note…

I pop outta the mattress.

Tear's lookin right at me. He says I've gotta go meet my guy. Get to where I'm getting.

I nod and I says to him Happy fuckin trails to ya, pal. I appreciate all the help you done for me.

Tear says Right back at you. Then he sticks out a hand for I'm supposed to shake it.

So I shake the fuckin hand, and it's some kinda special moment on accounta I got the reasonable certainties I ain't never gonna see this guy again. Goin to the fuckin Netherlands, after all, where do I bet he's gonna take a name ain't a fuckin homonoid for another word, or what do you call it, like tear and tear, when it's the same as a word what's different from the word what'd you wanna…anyway, that ain't what matters. What I'm sayin is, he's gonna change his name. And I don't figure he's gonna send me a postcard's got a little Dutch boy lickin a lollipop in a windmill on it what tells me what'd he change it to.

Tear and I finish shakin, and he turns to Howie and he says By the way, just in case the money being withheld doesn't keep you in line – I've still got my boys here in town. And mail crosses the Atlantic.

Yeah, it does! I think maybe I oughta ask him bout droppin me a postcard what's got a little Dutch boy lickin a lollipop in a windmill on it, only this don't seem like when's the best time would I do that. So I don't do that.

Tear keeps sayin You double cross my boy here, then the cash you don't have is gonna be the least of your problems.

Howie throws his hands up and says You don't have to threaten me! I agreed to help!

Tear says Yeah, out of the kindness of your heart, I know.

I says to Tear Golly fuckin gosh, I'm one of your boys now, huh?

Tear nods.

Howie says Real cute, fellas. Sorry you won't get to run off together. But I am gonna need some money now.

I says to him Keep dreamin, Howie.

Howie gets a little purple and he says *Howard*. Do you really not trust me? I'm gonna

Tear and I both interrupt him with we're sayin No.

Howie goes *more* purple, almost like Tear's givin his neck another hug, and he says I need to bribe some people. I don't have much of a, ah, a working relationship with the people who run the blocks.

I just nod at that, on accounta I know all bout the relationships ain't quite workin ones cept for how money makes the world go round.

Lucky for me, that ain't the only kind of relationship there is.

Tear turns to the door and says to me I'll get some more cash from the vault haul.

You believe that? Even though it ain't likely am I ever gonna get to pay him back what's he lendin Howie? Yeah, I guess it's outta my cut I ain't gettin anyway, but whatever. Just goes to fuckin show ya, they got good eggs in every fuckin henhouse.

I ain't afraid to say, I'm gonna miss that guy.

2

VEN ONCE IT'S GOT MOST of its fuckin stuffin back in, this thing still don't look like no mattress I ever fuckin zonked on. Good thing I don't say nothin suchwise, on accounta second thought I got is no shit, it's still got a me-sized hole in it.

I pick it up and I says Looks like if a mattress was a crab. Like it fuckin molted.

Howie don't say nothin to me. Now that Tear ain't here, he's gone all quiet on me. Ain't the kinda quiet makes me figure he's scared of me. Somethin kinda like the opposite of that, even.

I ain't lovin the fuckin silent treatment. So I says to Howie What size was this fuckin thing, prior to ya gutted it?

He sniffs and he says It was just a regular cot size.

In my head, I was figurin some kinda king size, luxurious fuckin trampoline of a mattress. Hindsight says that was fuckin dumb, on accounta the fuck is a prison gonna be doin with a fuckin luxury? Only I figure I figured that figure on accounta I couldn't wrap my head around how the fuck am I supposed to fit inside the sorta mattress I know full well ain't hardly big enough for me to lay on top of?

Howie musta seen what am I figurin carved into my fuckin facial region, on accounta he comes over and takes the mattress outta my hand and he says to me You have to go in sideways, like this. Then he starts to demonstrate, only he don't go all the way in, which I figure is on accounta maybe he's got some kinda fear I'm gonna bundle him up in it and swing him around over my head.

That's a thought what's funny to me, only I don't fuckin smile. On accounta I ain't in the smiletime mood.

I gotta say, it ain't like I'm fuckin scared of goin in. I ain't fond of tight spaces, between you and me, but I also ain't the sorta guy's gonna fuckin cry about. There ain't no fuckin tragic story from when was I a kid, like I got dropped into a well or some shit. I got nothin against small spaces, cept for my fuckin ribs. And that's where's my fuckin concern at. I'm a big guy. I gotta take big breaths. I got my nose broken so many times, most of the breaths gotta come in like gulps, mouthwise.

I'm sittin curled in the mattress, I ain't sure how's it not gonna look like the fuckin thing's just finished a long lap in the swimmin pool.

I relay this fuckin obstacle to Howie. He just shrugs and he says If somebody wanted to stand there and really *look* at the mattress, it'd be pretty goddamned obvious that there was something wrong with it. But nobody will. And it'll be dark, too. The only people we'd have to worry about seeing me bring you into the prison would be seeing from far, far away. Far enough that, even if they *wanted* to be a pain in the ass and start poking the mattress, which, you know, why *would* they, but even if they *did*, from up in the tower or on the walls, they're not gonna see how the mattress, which, you know, I'll be moving like a mattress, is or isn't like a normal mattress.

So I says to him And I can bust on out any time I need, right?

He nods and he says Yeah, but that's not a good thing. It'll be the easiest thing in the world for you to pop out, even by accident. Which means once you're stitched inside, you need to be very, *very* careful about how you move. Otherwise you might put a leg through the bottom right as I'm bringing you through the gate. Right where the night watch has eyes on you.

I fold my arms and frown at the dead mattress. I says How long I gotta be in there?

Howie says All told? Hour, hour and a half. I have to sew you in here, then we've gotta

I interrupt him and I wave my hands to say get a load of these fuckin whereabouts and I move my mouth to say How come you gotta sew me in *here?* Let's get on the road first, huh?

He looks at me like I'm a fuckin idiot and he says Where else do you think I can sew a large man into a mattress and *not* attract attention?

I says to him Fair play to ya. Go on.

He harrumphs and he says We get in the bed of the truck, I sew you in there, we drive to Sing Sing, go through, get you into storage...I'd say an hour and a half, if we really haul ass.

So I says But maybe two. Might be closer to two hours.

He says to me Your chum Tear did it. You think you can't do it?

I says Course I can fuckin do it, but that don't mean I gotta be singin a song over it.

Then I shake my head and I says to myself Ok.

Then I says to Howie Ok.

Then I grab the mattress and I says to Howie You wanna show me where's the fuckin truck already?

3

L ISTEN, I ain't a bashful guy. You probably figured that already. I ain't the sorta guy's gonna do somethin impressive and then say to ya Aw gee fuckin shucks, it wasn't nothin what I just done. If I done somethin ain't nothin, I ain't gonna pretend it weren't somethin. See what I'm sayin?

Like lemme real quick give ya a for instance. One time, this was when I set first foot in the city, prior to anybody's got a fuckin inklin what was gonna kick off in Sarajevo (well, at least no anybody I ever met), this lady's got a pram with her kid in it. She's walkin down the street with it, where to, I got no fuckin idea. Only she's some kinda klutz on accounta one second she's pushin the thing, next second it's rollin away from her and she's screamin. Now, it's rollin off the street part's for people, into the street part's still got horses clompin around. She's screamin about My baby, my baby! It's real fuckin dramatic.

So what do I do? Fuckin wet behind the ears Samuzzo D'Amato, new to town? I don't fuckin hesitate. I spring into fuckin action. Turns out, the action what'd I spring to maybe wasn't the best fuckin action. That's what'd the cops tell me later. The fuck do they know though, huh? They weren't there.

Anyway, what I do is I see this pram rollin towards the street, and I says to myself If I don't spring into fuckin action, that baby's gonna get smushed by the horsies. So I spring into the street, right in front of the horsie I figure's makin the most risk far as smushin goes, and I pop that horsie right in its fuckin snout. It gets real upset and falls asleep. The carriage it's been draggin tips with it, but that ain't my problem. The pram's my fuckin problem. I say as much to the stuffed shirts screamin at me from inside the carriage lyin on its side, I say Would you quit screamin at me, that ain't my fuckin problem!

The pram's still rollin though, so I go to the next horsie and I pop *that* son of a bitch on the nose. Down he goes. And trust me, it was a fuckin he. Ain't no mistakin.

Still, the pram's on a fuckin mission! So I go to the next horsie, pow, down it goes.

Two horsies after that, the lady catches up to the curb-jumpin crib and she yells at me Why didn't you stop it?

I says to her The fuck are you talkin about, I stopped five of em! And I point at the five horsies layin around in the square, in case she fuckin missed em.

She says My baby! Why didn't you stop my baby?!

I says to her I didn't figure it for a threat.

Only lookin at the horsies rollin around on the street, I figure maybe I didn't fuckin adjudge that so well.

Turns out a judge felt fuckin similar, only not the same. Tells me I gotta go to jail for a bit. I says to em Sure thing, only I gave em a fake name and they ain't never fuckin checked was it real or not, so course I never showed up, and they ain't never dunned me for it. So I figure that's on them.

I'm mentionin this by way of sayin, don't matter to me the lady didn't figure me a hero on accounta she had some real particular ideas about how do ya rescue a fuckin runaway newborn. I saved a baby, and I knocked out five horsies in a fuckin row. That's real impressive, and you gimme half the chance, I'll be the first fuckin guy says so.

Pride, ain't that what that is? I don't see why's it so fuckin bad. Too much ain't good, sure, but there ain't nothin stays good when you got too much of it. That's why's it *too much*. I figure, far as the prides go, I got just the right amount.

And it's that pride I got what's turnin out to be the

biggest fuckin problem here.

I'm a guy what clobbers horses and flips cars and unscrews people's feets. I ain't a guy gets sewn into a fuckin mattress. So how's it I'm gettin sewn into a fuckin mattress now? I ain't that sorta guy. Only I figure I gotta be, on accounta I'm gettin sewn into a fuckin mattress.

I curl in like how'd Howie tell me I gotta. Crunchin over my legs, squarin my hips and shoulders to the top of the mattress while's my back flush on the floor, best I can. Howie pushes in some extra fuckin stuffin on the side I crawled through and he asks me You good?

I says to him This is fuckin goofy. I ain't happy bout this fuckin goofy stratagem.

I hear Howie whisperin to himself, only I can't make out what's he sayin on accounta the cotton's fuckin dampin the sounds down. I can't see him neither, course. Just a load of fuckin puffywhite.

I says to him You got a new pal out there I oughta meet, Howie?

Howie says to me louder, he says *Howard*. And I just... I don't want to sew you in unless you *tell* me to.

Another jab right to the fuckin pride. I says to him Fuckin fine! Zip me up, doc! Let's just get fuckin movin so's I can get outta this fuckin thing!

I hear Howie sayin Ok ok ok. Then the puffywhite starts tremblin around me. The needle goin in and out, in and out, or however the fuck stitchin works on somethin ain't humans.

Can't help but wonder if this is fuckin worth it. Sure, I ain't rarin to spend my life livin as a fuckin fugitive, havin to be lookin over both fuckin shoulders at once, worryin about am I gonna get extradized even if I'm somewhere else in the fuckin world. That don't seem too fuckin appealin to me. But that's the fuckin life I got laid out for me. And the only way I got to roll that life up tight and suggest to the lady with the deli scales where can she stuff it is, I gotta lay here, like a bump on a log, only at least the bump's got some fuckin fresh air, while I just gotta lay here and get stitched into a fuckin mattress.

Two hours in a mattress for a lifetime of bein a free bird, and even still, I'm wonderin, is it fuckin worth it? Pride-wise? This ain't somethin I can take back. I'm always gonna be the guy what let himself get sewed into a mattress. That'll be a fuckin thing I gotta live with. Bein a fugitive gives ya credibility, at least. Who the fuck's gonna take me seriously? Watch out, here comes Mr. Mattress! What a laugh.

But you know what it all comes down to? Oh, yeah, life with Daff, no doubt about that. Takin her to the opery or what the fuck, without I gotta try hidin who am I. That's got a spot on the fuckin marquee. But no, I was thinkin just then when'd I ask you what does it all come down to, I was thinkin bout that whole fuckin branzino. That's one thing I ain't gonna be able to get so easy, if I'm on the top of the FBI's fuckin wish list. Raheeq, he's a good guy, but he ain't dumb. He knows I ain't the most law-abidin fucker he ever gave a fish to. But outta respect, I don't break no fuckin laws when am I in his establishment. He didn't even gotta ask me, that's just somethin I done for him. Or not done, I figure.

But if me just *bein* in his establishment's breakin a law…I don't figure I'm ever gonna get that whole fuckin branzino again. In my life.

That ain't doin.

So alright, then. I'll be Mr. Fuckin Mattress.

I hear Howie ask me How're ya doin in there?

I'll tell ya, he's got better fuckin bedside manner than I figured he would. Get it? I'm a fuckin bed now!

I says to him All kinds of swell in here.

He says to me Alright. You need anything before we get going?

I got a lot of fuckin comedy answers, only I don't figure we got time for this no more. Take out the drive time, I figure there ain't much more'n an hour prior to I gotta be back in the bed in my fuckin cell. *On* the bed, I oughta specifize.

So I says to him I don't want for naught, Howie. Let's get.

He says to me *Howard!* And he slams the fuckin tailgate up.

4

OWIE'S GOT A TRUCK. The kind's got a back's exposed to the fuckin elements. A whaddyacall-it. Pickup? A pickup. Howie's got a pickup.

Seein as I'm a fuckin mattress now, there ain't room for me in the part where do the people sit. So I gotta be layin down in the back, exposed to the fuckin elements. And seein as it's the warm months, the elements are fuckin hot. And I'm wearin a goddamned mattress.

I'm really mentionin all that specialwise so you don't figure I'm sweatin like I am on accounta I'm fuckin nervous. It's the fuckin elements.

I am sweatin, though. Makin the cotton go all soggy, so's I'm just stewin in soggy cotton, and I'm layin in the back gettin jounced by the fuckin road, and I got nobody who can I talk to on accounta Howie's up where the people sit and I'm back here where you put the guys what're mattresses. Normally that ain't a problem for me, not havin nobody who can I talk to. I mean, I'm naturally fuckin garrulous, and if people don't like talkin to me they know better than sayin so. But I ain't no stranger to bein alone with my thoughts. Frankly it's nice to get em on their own sometimes, on accounta that way if one of the rotten ones has an unfortunate accident, there ain't no witnesses.

But normalwise I ain't alone with my thoughts inside a fuckin mattress what's gotta be three hundred fuckin degrees. Bakin me like a goddamned branzino, how you like that? And I'm back here figurin, I got no way of seein are we actually goin the right way, I got no way of knowin how long til we get where're we goin, and even when we get where're we goin, I gotta hold still and keep fuckin mum, no matter how much I'm gettin moved, til Howie says to me Come on out.

I don't give a shit how tight you figure you got your head screwed on, that ain't a place nobody can be in without their thoughts start to turn on em.

We hit a big fuckin bump gets me airtime, then *whaps* me back down into the fuckin bed of the truck. Lemme tell ya, the truck bed ain't soft like the kinda bed I am. It's got splinters and a bad fuckin attitude.

You wanna know who do I respect most in this whole fuckin debacle? My girl, Daff. Even when I ain't treatin her like I oughta, she sees it's only on accounta I ain't got the aptitude. Ain't a case where she's wonderin on my intentions. As I'm fuckin reflectin on it, I figure it's on accounta sometimes I scramble up the doin and the bein. Which I'm sayin to say, doin somethin nice for somebody ain't the same as *bein* somethin nice for somebody. And sometimes bein means you maybe ain't doin, just at the moment.

Somethin to fuckin figure on. Between *whap*s.

5

OULD BE I'm only layin here gettin *whapped* for an hour and then some. Might be I'm here for seven years. I got no frame of fuckin reference. Bedframe. Fuck me. Anyway, a real long time after Howie stitched me up back here, the truck stops.

First thing makes me figure somethin ain't right is, the truck stops *hard*. Til now, I figure Howie was doin his best to be some kinda fuckin ginger with the wheel. Ginger like soft'n fuckin easy, not like Wally's ain't-a-sister. Or the spice, but weren't nobody talkin bout the spice til you just brought it up. Boy, I'm some kinda fuckin hungry.

This time though, Howie fuckin *slams* on the brakes. The car squeals, I slide right up and get some fuckin splinters in my back, *through the fuckin mattress*, and bonk my noggin on the back of the fuckin whaddyacallit. Where do the people sit in the truck. Pardon *me* for I can't come up with the fuckin word, I just got bonked by it.

I hear somebody shoutin. Somebody ain't Howie. I figure they're kinda far away, only distance is like time, far as not havin no frame of fuckin reference in here.

Yeah, I wanna rip myself outta the fuckin mattress, on accounta I wanna see who's yellin about what from where. Only the thing is, it ain't like there's a fuckin zipper, or some buttons. I bust outta the mattress, it's gonna have a big fuckin rip in it. And I got no clue did Howie bring his sewin kit with him. The mattress gets a rip, I gotta figure the whole plan goes up. Or down. Won't work, wherever it fuckin goes.

But the yellin's gettin louder. Sounds to me like closer.

I hear Howie's door open, but it don't close. I can feel it doin a little dance on his side while's he movin around though, so I figure he's hangin out the driverside door now. Little guy weighs more'n I figured, maybe, judgin by how's he knockin the fuckin truck around.

Howie yells somethin sounds to me like Get out of the fucking road! He yells it the way you yell at a brother what's razzin ya. That's a fuckin assumption on accounta I ain't never had a brother, but I been razzed, and I yelled at the folks what did it. Sounded kinda like how's Howie soundin, with the Ha ha actually means You better cut that shit out.

So the little guy's got more spunk than what'd I figure, too!

Judgin from the way the truck rocks, I figure Howie just got outta the cab. Cab! That was the word I couldn't remember on accounta I bonked it.

Whoever's in the fuckin road yells somethin at Howie. Yells it in a way *don't* sound like razzin. Sounds like hot fuckin blood.

I hiss at Howie Hey Howie, you bring your fuckin needlepoints?

He says to me his real name, then he says No. Don't get out of the mattress.

Then he says Oop and gets back in the truck, *real* fast. Slammin his door *hard*.

Then I hear a fuckin *pop* from where was the voice comin from.

Then I hear a *thnk* from a place on the truck just got hit by a fuckin bullet.

Even through the back wall of the cab, I can hear Howie go Eek!

I says to Howie The fuck's goin on out there?!

Only Howie can't hear me on accounta he's revvin up the engine. He guns it, pedal down on the fuckin metal.

Good news is, the truck's got better pickup than I fuckin figured. The pickup's got pickup. Ha.

That's the bad news too though, is that what's got the pickup is a pickup, and somebody ain't done a great job of latchin up the back.

So what happens is sorta like rippin the tablecloth out from under some fine fuckin china. The whole truck tears down the road, and Mr. Mattress here, he just sits where he is til there ain't no truck under him anymore.

As in, I slide right out the fuckin back.

Second good news is since my head was gettin bonked on the cab, it's my feet go out first. So it's my feet hit the ground, which I fuckin realize as my head-side slides off the bed means I'm about to get *whap* yep there's the ground, and now I got a fuckin headache.

I figure Howie ain't noticed I came off the back, on accounta I can hear the truck screamin off down the road.

So now I'm just a mattress in the middle of the fuckin road, in the middle of fuckin nowhere, in the middle of the fuckin night.

And there's some kinda gun guy prowlin around out there.

So look, I know bustin outta the mattress is gonna make gettin in to Sing Sing a hell of a lot harder. But the situation's fuckin changed. It's one thing, bein a mattress with a plan. But what, I'm gonna be a mattress in the middle of the road, just *hopin* Howie figures out I ain't in his fuckin truck no more? Uh-uh. I don't think so.

I punch through the fuckin fluffypuffy and rip it right down the middle.

6

UST GOTTA STRESS THIS real hard at the top: I *ain't cryin.* But, I'm only gonna say, I get why do babies cry right after they rip through their mama's fluffypuffy. I gotta imagine it's a similar fuckin experience to this: you're layin there for so long, not doin nothin much with your time but bein alone with your little thoughts, then all of a sudden you're out, and you ain't totally sure where the fuck are you or what's goin on, and there's this guy with a gun standin in a ditch by the side of the road.

Real fuckin disorientin, lemme tell ya.

Takes me a second to put together, but the guy with the gun is fuckin Gephen. The Paci-FIST fuck what'd start brawlin with Tear. Which was where'd all my fuckin problems tonight start, if you ain't countin I broke outta Sing Sing as where'd the problems start.

Anyhow, Gephen's just standin there starin at me, on accounta I guess he didn't figure a bruiser was gonna self-cesarean outta the fuckin mattress what just fell outta the truck.

I says to Gephen The fuck are you doin here, aside from ruinin my fuckin reverse prison break?

Gephen shouts at me What are *you* doing?

I says to him I just fuckin said to you, I was doin a reverse prison break!

He says to me Why were you fucking in a mattress?

THE WHOLE BRANZINO

I start walkin towards him, real slow, hands up. Tryin to make a point of I ain't lookin at that fuckin gun what'm I gonna snatch from him. I says You ain't never heard that expression, about goin to the mattresses?

He does some crazy eyebrow shit at me. Then he says That's not what it means!

I says to him Oh, *now* you tell me! Hey, you been cryin or what?

Gephen points the gun at me and he says I have *not* been crying!

I shrug on accounta I ain't quite in gun-snatchin distance yet, so I ain't lookin to get him too wound up. So I says to him What're you doin out here, pal?

Gephen ain't lowerin the gun. He says to me Where's Tear?

I says to him He's on his way to the land of fuckin funny-color bulb flowers.

Gephen points the gun at me harder and he says Stop coming closer! Stay fucking where you are!

I ain't in a position where am I gonna lindy hop outta the path of a fuckin bullet, so I do what does Gephen suggest. Then I says to him I ain't got time for this, guy. You just fucked my reverse prison break, so I gotta

He interrupts me so's he can ask me Where's Tear? While he asks he's lookin all around like the guy must be hidin in the fuckin bushes.

I says to him You got listenin problems or what? On accounta I already said to you, *he ain't here.* Now you wanna quit pointin that fuckin gun at me?

Gephen keeps on pointin the fuckin gun at me.

Wind tousles the fuckin treetops on either side of the road, like they're a little kid what're they proud of for hittin a home run or some shit.

Gephen says to me Tear was going to help you break back in to

I says to him Yeah, he fuckin did. Then I point at where'd Howie's truck go and I says to Gephen That was how'd Tear help me, is settin up that fuckin farce with the mattress. Which you just went and ruined, you fuckin bozo.

Clear as day, Gephen's havin a hell of time processin what am I sayin. Gets even clearer on accounta he asks me This is the only road you could have taken. He has to be here.

I says to him If wishes were horses or somethin, ain't that a phrase?

He says Tear killed my best friend.

I says Yeah, I heard about that.

He says So *where the hell is he?*

I says Your friend? Well I hear good little boys go to heaven, so I wouldn't start lookin there.

Gephen steps up to me, gun leadin the way, and he says NOT MY FRIEND! *WHERE'S TEAR?!*

He stops at a spot's still just outta my fuckin reach. I could try for the gun…only I ain't the sprightliest son of a bitch you ever met, and I ain't so clear on how quick're Gephen's reflexives.

And anywise, now that I'm closer, I can see he's a big fuckin guy. Bigger'n me, if you can get your fuckin gourd around such a thing. Ain't like I don't figure I could win a bout of fuckin fisticuffs, only it might take longer'n how long do I got. Could be some of the guards in Sing Sing are already up and fixin their fuckin coffee, pickin up yesterday's paper and flippin right through to the funny pages.

So I keep just where I am. Calm as can be, I says to him Like I fuckin said to ya, he's on a boat somewhere, goin to some other somewhere's gonna get him to an even further fuckin somewhere. And I got no way of sniffin out where is he, or even givin him a ring-a-ding. I don't got shit for ya, Gephen. He's gone, and he ain't comin back. So quit pointin that pea shooter at me, huh?

Gephen takes all that on board real slow. Like it's iced cream he's tryin to suck through a straw, only it's gotta melt prior to he can give himself brain freeze.

Then he lowers the gun, and he goes all slouchy, and he mopes at me, he mopes It's just fucking not *fair*. I wanted

I don't give a shit what's he sayin, and I ain't fond of he's still holdin the gun, so I duck my head and barrel towards him, shoulder-first.

He shouts at me to let me know he noticed I'm barrelin towards him, then he squeezes off a shot at me. I got no clue where does it go, only I know it don't hit me. So I keep runnin, then my shoulder meets his fuckin ribs. He squeezes off another shot when're we halfway to the dirt, and I'm here hopin it don't blow up a fuzzy owl or whoever the fuck lives in them trees there. Pretty sure they got owls out here.

Thwack, I use Gephen to break my fuckin descent. I

put a hand on his throat and lean, tellin him Relax. Cut it out.

Gephen's fightin under me. He ain't such a menace once I got him pinned, but I ain't lookin to let him get back on his feet.

I says to him Would you drop the fuckin gun already?

Not only does he not do what'd I suggest, he starts crankin his wrist so's the fuckin gun's pointin at me!

I take my right hand off his neck, and I sock him once on the nose, then a second time on the nose, then I put my hand back on his neck and I use my left hand to grab his right wrist, on accounta that's the hand's got the gun in it, and I start smashin it into the dirt.

Boy, he's got a hell of a grip on that thing!

Speakin of, he reaches up with that other hand of his and jams his thumb in my fuckin eye.

I says Aaaaaah!

He says Grrrrraaaaah!

I take my right hand off his neck and use it to swat away his mit what's inconveniencin my peeper.

Now we each got a free hand, and we're just sorta slappin at each other with em. While I'm still usin the other one to try to smash the gun outta his fuckin grip.

Then I remember about this big fuckin bologna block I call my noggin, and I have gravity give me a hand with I'm smashin my fuckin forehead into his face.

Gotta be honest, that slows *both* of us down some. Only I was the one seen it comin, so I'm first to lose the fuckin tweetie birds around my head. I elbow him hard in the jaw, then

SHIT. He fuckin juked outta the way.

And he fuckin rolls me. So I'm the one's flat on my back, and he's puttin his knee in *my* fuckin ribs. How'd that happen?

Goin for the fuckin what's he ain't gonna see comin, I wrap my legs around his fuckin torso and squeeze.

He grunts and starts tryin to stand, which brings my fuckin lower body up with him. Like he's deadliftin my corpus. This guy's got some fuckin muscle, lemme tell ya!

Only I ain't lookin to tender him such a compliment, on accounta how he jams that fuckin gun what's he got into my face and pulls the trigger.

The gun says to us *click*.

Gephen quits fightin for a second to make a surprise face at his firearm.

I quit fightin for a second just to double check I ain't dead. Then I'm just mad as hell about this fucker tried to fuckin shoot my fuckin face off.

Guess his gun's takin my side here. Misfire or outta bullets. Either way, bully for me.

So I do a fuckin situp while do I still got him in a leg hug, turnin that situp into another fuckin headbutt. He goes back flat on his ass, and now we're just sittin across from each other like we're settin up to play patty cake. Only instead of that I grab hold of his nose and twist that fuckin thing like an egg timer, and I can feel his skin start to fuckin tear at the bridge.

Gotta make a mental note to say somethin sharp about *here's that Tear you was lookin for, in terms of I'm tearin your face off*, if I can get some fuckin air in my lungs without too much time's passed so he wouldn't get it.

Figure Gephen felt about his face startin to rip too, on accounta he drops the gun and puts both his hands up.

That easifies my fuckin job of calmin this fuckin guy down. Few more socks and pops around the face and fuckin torso, then I got Gephen back on the ground where's he fuckin belong. This time, I'm kneelin on his fuckin neck.

I says to Gephen I made myself a mental fuckin note to say somethin to you, only I can't figure which of my fuckin brain drawers did I stick that in.

He don't say nothin to that, just kicks at the fuckin dirt.

I says Oh well. Anywise, I think I mentioned prior to you decided you wanted to get your ass kicked, but you just fucked up my reverse prison break. So here's what's what. You got a car tucked behind a bush or somethin out here?

I ease up on him enough so's he can say Yes!

I says to him Swell. So here are the two fuckin paths what do you got to choose from. Either you take me to your car and you help me figure out how am I gonna get back into the big house, or I pull your head off and throw it hard as I can at a tree.

He don't think about it too long, he just says Take my car.

I says to him Uh-uh. This ain't the sorta thing I'm gonna work out on my lonesome. Path one is, you gotta help. Might be you could do a fuckin look-at-me, a whad-dyacallit. On accounta it ain't gonna be as big a deal if you get spotted.

Gephen looks down at himself. Bigger than me, you recall I said to ya. So he says to me If I get spotted, they'll probably just assume I *am* supposed to be inside, and throw me in!

I says to him Maybe you shoulda thoughta that prior to you fucked up my mattress plan.

He asks me How was I fucking supposed to know you had a mattress plan?!

So I says Maybe that's what you shoulda thoughta!

Then I start thinkin to myself, how am I gonna trust this fuckin guy? Gonna be hard enough figurin how am I gonna get back into Sing Sing without I'm sweatin Gephen gettin behind me.

I start makin a real persuasive fuckin case to myself about how I oughta just kill him. Could be I can still get a look-at-me, *god* what's the fuckin word I'm tryin for there? Conversion? No. When you're tryin to make folks quit lookin at the crime you're doin, so you set up some-thin big what do they feel like they *gotta* look at instead, like a convent car wash. Buncha nuns washin cars. That ain't a real example what I ever been a part of, no clue why is that what jumped outta my fuckin brain there.

I gotta figure somethin on my facials says to Gephen about how am I thinkin it might be I oughta just kill him, on accounta he starts sayin I'll help. I'll help you out.

I says to him What I need is help *in*.

He says Sure. That.

Now I ain't figurin I *am* gonna kill him. I just ain't wholly settled on either side of that fuckin white picket. So I just look at him, see what else does he gotta say.

What's he gotta say is Hang on a second. Then he tries to stand up, only I got my knee on him like I mentioned. Then he says I'll help you!

I says to him How? What do you got?

He says Whatever, I can help however! I'll help. Now he's got panic in his voice and wet in his eyes what tells me he knows I'm the one's gonna choose does he keeps suckin air or not.

Me before I did all them Paci-FIST meetins, I bet I'd have just detached this guy's fuckin braincase. He took a fuckin shot at me, remember that? More'n one, come to think of it. And here I am, thinkin about ain't there a way to do this without havin to kill this asshole.

You know what? I'm just gonna say it, I'm some kinda swell fuckin fella.

Just to discourage this fuckin guy from tryin to get the jump on me, I says to him I'm gonna get off ya now, and here's the deal. We got nothin personal between us. That scrape we had just now was all a misunderstandin. Bygones under the bridge, you see what I'm sayin. So you got no cause to jump me. But sure as that, you ain't got no cause to help me neither. So I'm sayin, I got five grand comin your way if you help me out with this. Okay?

Gephen says Okay! Okay! Only he says it in a way makes me figure he's only tryin to get me off him. He ain't actually heard what'd I say. Which don't bode well for our fuckin collaboration.

THE WHOLE BRANZINO

So I don't get off him. Instead I'm lookin around the woods, seein what do we got to work with. We got woods, and we got the flesh of a fuckin mattress what's been all shredded up. I gotta figure even once Howie clocks I ain't on the back of his truck anymore, he ain't comin back. So that's all we got there, is the woods and the mattress flesh.

And I got Gephen. Who, soon as I get off him, I got some kinda confidence is gonna try to jump me. Just his nature. Clockwork bruiser like him, he don't got the logics and cunnings the way I do. Which, bein fair, neither do I. I'm just pals with Wally.

I'm just about talkin myself into I really *oughta* kill this guy, just so he don't have a chance to fuckin jump me, only from the way how'd I say *I'm just about* you know I ain't gonna do that.

On accounta I figure I got a way how can Gephen help.

I look out at all the trees, then back at the ripped-up mattress, then back at Gephen.

He says to me You were gonna get off me, you said?

And I says to him I figure I got a way how can you help.

He says …okay.

I says You probably ain't gonna like it.

He frowns but don't say No.

I ask him Which is your best leg?

He says My best…?

I ask him You're right handed, right? Is what I figure from how'd you hold the gun.

He says to me …Yeah?

So I says to him Alrighty, I'll break your left leg then. Then I hop to it. And by that I mean, on it.

7

SAYS TO MYSELF Tee hee hee, on accounta it's pretty fuckin funny. Then I'm gettin closer to the prison so I figure I gotta quit gigglin.

I creep to the next bush over, so now I'm, I don't know, a couple hundred feet from the gate goes into the fuckin jail. Ain't nothin to hide behind, between this bush and that gate. Just flat fuckin pavement. Then once you're through the gate, you got another gate behind it. Chain link, tall like three of me. Problem is, it's gettin near enough into tomorrow that it's just fuckin today now. I ain't even talkin bout how I probably got half a fuckin hour, if that, for gettin back in my cell. I'm just sayin how the mornin's goin from black to blue. Visibility, is what I'm sayin. Meanwhile I got two fences I gotta get through, and I still ain't wholly sure how'm I gonna get through gate number two. But I do got some designs on how'm I gonna get through gate number one.

Good ol Gephen, he's gonna fuckin open er up for me.

This is fuckin foolproof here. A plan I came up with all on my own. I can't wait til when do I tell Wally and Godric and them about this, they're gonna say *wow, what a great fuckin whaddyacallit, good thinkin Sammy.*

Yeah, there ain't nothin stoppin Gephen from turnin tail and limpin off into the night, cept for how'd I say I'd give him money if he helped me and I'd fuckin kill him if he didn't.

Looks like I'm out the cash, then, on accounta I see him staggerin outta the woods now, into the clearin what's the prison got outside its gates.

I sees him and I says Ha ha ha, on accounta he looks fuckin ridiculous.

What I did after I snapped his second-best leg was, I ripped up the mattress flesh some more, then I draped it on him. Scuffed him up a bit, stuck some cotton to him, then I told him Off ya fuckin go. Which is where's he fuckin goin now, is off, so's he can call for help from the guards, tellin em he was out campin and he got mauled by a fuckin bear, can he come inside and have some cocoa and call his ma.

I'm figurin, ain't a crime to get lost in the woods and ask the maximum security prison what do ya stumble upon for help, is it? Maybe it ain't the thing's most likely to fuckin happen, but there ain't no law against it, right?

Point of fact, I got no clue is that true or not. But I said to Gephen I knew for a fact there weren't no law against it, on accounta I didn't want him gettin the fuckin jitters prior to he's goin up to the gate.

I watch him limpin and scrapin, covered in dirt and fluff and mattress flesh. First I figure he's hammin it up like he figures somebody's gonna be handin out awards at the end, then I remember about how I done a *real* good job, far as snappin his second-best leg goes.

I further fuckin realize maybe that weren't quite fuckin necessary, on accounta the rest of him looks so fucked up we ain't got a need for quite that much quote verisimilitude unquote. And what kinda hard-boiled bear is this supposed to be he met, what skips the claws and just starts crunchin bones?

So then I feel a little fuckin rotten for figurin he looks some kinda ridiculous, like a ghost slug slimin over concrete. Only that gets me laughin again on accounta slugs got ghosts now.

I says to myself Maybe I oughta had him pretend like the bear fuckin ate him, and he's a ghost. Have him go up sayin Oooooooh, I'm a fuckin ghost.

My brain says to me Ghosts aren't real.

I says to my brain I fuckin know they ain't real, I'm just sayin, mighta been funny.

So my brain says The point isn't to make us laugh, it's to get them to open the gate.

I says to my brain The fuck you keep tellin me things I already know for? I'm the one's gotta get through the fuckin gate. You're just the fuckin jockey, bouncin along up top.

My brain says I'm keeping you company. I want to make sure you get in alright.

Then I frown on accounta I was bein a rat and I says to my brain That's real decent of ya. I fuckin appreciate that, you bein a pal.

My brain just waves away the nice thing what'd I say, which is sorta how some tough guys tell ya Thanks.

So we both of us watch Gephen limpin up to the gate.

He looks back at us.

My brain and I both flap our arms at him, sayin Don't look at us, ya fuckin jelly roll!

He keeps lookin back at us all confused. Which is how I recall I ain't actually here with my brain. I mean, I *am,* only it ain't...I am my fuckin brain. My brain is me. So who the fuck was I talkin to there?

I'll figure that out later, on accounta Gephen grabs hold of the fence and starts rattlin it. We can...*I* can kinda hear he's yellin for Anybody home, that sorta thing.

I look over at the slice of sky where's it startin to blush about oh my god oh my god here comes the mornin. And I start wonderin, usin my brain I'm wonderin, do they actually got bears in New York here? I figure they do, only...maybe I oughta said to Gephen he oughta hedge a bit, far as what'd he get mauled by goes. Maybe I oughta said owl, on accounta I do figure they got those here.

Corner of my eye, I see three guards got their shit together now, they're openin the second gate so's they can get to the first and tell Gephen You're way ahead of yourself for the fuckin trick or treat times.

You know...I was some kinda confident bout this plan when was it just a plan. Now that it's a thing that's happenin...I ain't feelin quite so strong on it. Gephen and I ain't come up with no details for how come he was out here cept for *campin.* Could be they'll ask him for some fuckin details beyond *campin,* to check is this bruiser on the up-and-up, on accounta most guys our size ain't. And seein how I ain't actually needed to lean that hard on Gephen prior to he starts gettin the watery eyes...

I figure this mighta been the wrong play here.

So I says to myself Fuck this, and I start creepin around towards the back of the prison. Nearer to where'd I land when I broke outta the fuckin place.

As I'm goin, though, I get another look at Gephen, and I start chucklin again. Then I'm circlin round to the back, gigglin like a fuckin kid just found where does daddy hide the moonshine.

8

ONCE I GET AROUND THE BACK, I ain't gigglin no more. On accounta yeah I know I can climb the fences back here, only what am I lookin at on the other side of em but solid fuckin wall, and a door here or there looks like it's gotta be six inches thick, of fuckin steel or somethin. Not to mention, there ain't no trees to hide in back here. I'm out in the goddamned open.

My brain says to me Well, we're back here now, while our what-do-you-call-it is playing itself out round the front. What's the move?

I says to my brain You again, huh? Well Jesus, it ain't like you put the kibosh on we're comin back here. You got just as much info on what're we workin with here, prison doors-wise, as I got. You went here too.

My brain says to me *Went here?* Like it's an elementary school?

I says You know what am I sayin.

My brain says *Went here.*

I says Alright, quit it with the went here.

Then I look up and I see the fuckin hole in the wall where'd I jump outta. My fuckin cell, right there. Close and far at the same second. It's some kinda fuckin high up, lemme tell ya. Can't believe I made it down. I musta really wanted that whole branzino, jumpin out a window what's that high up!

All of a sudden Sing Sing starts makin good on its name. It's goin AWOOOOOOOOGAH with some kinda volume behind it.

I smile and I says to my brain I don't figure things are goin so hot for ol Gephen over there.

My brain kinda grimaces inside my head and he says That's bad for us too. Especially you.

I says How do you figure? Only I gotta shout it on accounta I can't barely hear myself over the fuckin alarm. So I says to my brain Havin a second thought about it, I take your fuckin point. Only I don't see how's it gonna be worse for me than you, on accounta we're the same guy.

My brain scratches my chin about our fuckin dilemma, and he says I mean, here's the thing. Whatever Gephen was doing, it didn't work. In a big way. So Sing Sing's got its pique up. It's gonna be that much harder to get in.

Then he kinda tilts my head and curls my nose and he

says So you really have two options here. You can try to find a way in and risk getting caught, which will leave you even worse off than you were before…or you can accept the life of a fugitive.

I ask him You mean book it?

He nods.

I says to him And kiss the whole branzino goodbye?

He says Uh…I mean, among other things, yeah.

I shake my head and I says Fuck that. I'm gettin in. Question's how.

He says It's a hell of a question.

I says Like, how hard can it be?

He says Pretty hard.

I says to him No, *how 'ard* can it be?

He says …

So I says *Howard* can

He interrupts me and says Howard. I get it. Howard.

I says Howard can it be.

He says *I get it.* That's a lot easier said than done though, even the way you say it.

I says to him Oh yeah?

He says Yeah. How are we gonna reconnect with him?

So I says Well I was figurin first off, I wave to him like fuckin thusly. Then I raise my hand and I wave at Howard, who's pokin his head over the wall hissin about where the fuck did I go.

All I'm wonderin is, how the fuck did my brain not see him?

THE WHOLE BRANZINO

9

I GO MEET HOWIE at the door what he hissed at me I oughta meet him at. Well, I meet him at the gate's in front of the door. He comes and gets me, swingin his head around the whole time like it's a magic eight ball ain't givin him the answer he wants.

Then he walks me through the gate, then through the door. And I'm back in. I'm back in fuckin Sing Sing. With the white painted walls and ceilins what're too low. Still gotta make it to my cell, but hey, this is pretty fuckin good, right? Even if I biff it here, at least I can look at my eyes in my prison mirror what ain't made of glass and say Well buddy, you got close. Missed the cigar by *that much,* or what do people say about that.

I frown on accounta if I biff it here, they'd build a new fuckin prison just for me. Solitary, I'd bet heavy on that. Assumin they ain't lookin to just fry me.

This here's the point of no fuckin return. Goin on the lam, livin as a fugitive, that was a choice I coulda made prior to now. Not anymore, though. Now I gotta see this through, or kiss the fuckin sunshine goodbye.

So I'm gettin some kinda antsy, and meanwhile I got Howie doin nothin for my fuckin mood by he's askin me again where the fuck did I go.

I remind him about I oughta be askin *him* that, on accounta he was the one what had wheels, whereas I was a fuckin bedroom essential.

He just says to me *Bah* on accounta he's some kinda fuckin stressed. From the sound of it he got one hell of a sermon from his superior, bout showin up when he ain't supposed to and why's he doin that when he can't even get to his fuckin shifts on time, on accounta I bet he shows up late to work.

I says to him You showin up late to work?

He just tells me I don't want to talk about my god-damned work attendance records right now.

He stops us at a fuckin four-corners in the hall. Then we're walkin again, and Howie really lets *me* have it, on accounta somebody let *him* have it and it's a law of fuckin nature that when somebody's had to really have it from somebody else, that first somebody what really had it is gonna turn around and let somebody *else* really have it, on accounta pride or some shit. It's like fuckin hot potato, only the music ain't never gonna stop, and it's been playin from time fuckin in memoriam. I bet it goes all the way back to one cave guy says to another cave guy You were supposed to have that fire started twenty minutes ago! Just really lettin him have it, ooga-booga style. And so then the second cave guy turns around and really lets this other cave guy have it, yellin about Who said you could draw a hairy elephant on my wall?! And ever since then it's just been the same *it* what's everybody really lettin each other have, crossin the globe til we got wars what you gotta ride a boat to go fight in. And now it's Howie's the one's really lettin me have it. A gift from fuckin loincloth times, without the receipt.

He snarls at me That moron who started trying to

climb the gate, wasn't that the asshole who ambushed us? On the road? And you brought him *in* on this?! Everyone's losing their minds in here now, because they're not stupid, they're assuming he was meant to be a diversion from *something*, so everybody's

I says to him Fuck me, *diversion!*

He shows me his forehead.

I says to him Couldn't recall that word earlier. What were you sayin?

He says to me Everybody's on high alert now, but if you'd been smart and patient and just done what I fucking told you to do, we wouldn't be

Now I'm all for lettin somebody steam emselves out, only I ain't gonna stand for a guy's twistin the how-was-it so much. So I interrupt him and I says to him Done what you said? I don't remember you sayin nothin about gunnin it so hard I go slidin out the back.

He says Well I *also* didn't say anything about us getting ambushed! And neither did you!

Real calm, I says to him Why don't we let's figure out what the fuck you're tryin to mean by that.

Someone walks into the hall we're walkin down. Howie pushes me back and down a different hall don't lead much of anywhere, far as I can tell. Given how do our relative sizes stack up, I oughta underline how'd I *let* myself get pushed.

Watchin the hall to see is the guy what popped out in front of us gonna come pokin in here or what, Howie whispers to me I'm not trying to mean anything. I'm just saying, you seemed to know who that guy was. Which makes me think you knew, on some level, that there was a chance of him ambushing us. It would have been really

I says to him The fuck are you talkin about, I seemed to know who was the guy? I was in the fuckin mattress. You were three fuckin counties over by the time I figured out who was the guy.

Howie says You know what I mean.

So I says I know you're *bein* mean, on accounta your boss really let you have it. How bout you quit fuckin takin it out on me? How bout that?

He's quiet while the fuckin interloper in the hall interlopes past us. Then Howie leads me back out into the where were we goin and we keep on our ain't-so-merry way. Then Howie says to me What do you want, an apology?

I says Now that you mention it, that'd go a way towards patchin up our fuckin friendship.

Howie says to me We don't *have* a friendship.

I says So we're gonna need a lot of fuckin patches, huh?

He sighs and don't say nothin, which I figure for a step towards fuckin cordial.

I figure I got a chance of gettin him the rest of the way there with fuckin flattery, which is good as fuckin currency to fellas don't deserve it, so I says to him So boss, where we goin?

Howie purses his lips like he loves bein called *boss* so much he wants to kiss the air what brought him the word. Then he says You were third floor, C ward, right?

I laugh and I ask him Hey, who the fuck you callin a

c-word?

He gives me eyes got so much fuckin disappointment in em, I says to him the word Sorry prior to my brain's even figured what's that feelin its feelin. Then I says Yeah, third floor, C ward, you got it.

Howie smiles and he says Then we're home free. Then he reaches into his pocket and he pulls out a fuckin key.

I ask him Is that the key to my cell you got there?

He smiles and nods and says Courtesy of Tear.

I have a quick look around and I ask him The fuck's Tear doin here?

Howie takes a real deep breath and he says The bribe money.

I says to him Oh yeah. Then I says Alright! And I thump him on the shoulder and then I further says See? You went and got that key even though you ain't had the slightest clue am I gonna get here or not. You wanna tell me that ain't *some* kinda fuckin friendship?

He shrugs and he says I imagined you'd make it here eventually. I'm doing this for the ten grand.

I says Sure ya are pal. Buddy. Chum.

He says Alright, cut it out.

I says to him Oh! Is that a fuckin smile I see there?

He says to me No. Only I can see a fuckin smile there!

Then we're quiet on accounta we're sneakin into the part of the prison's got all the bad boys in it, in the ward where they're gonna know who am I from my fuckin mug. Howie might be a pal what's got a case of the denials, but don't neither of us wanna see him get made as my fuckin accomplice.

10

W **E TIPTOE UP** and there it is. My fuckin cell. There's me, sleepin in bed, made of plaster, rat nibblin on my ear. Even though it's just the fake me's gettin chomped, I gotta say, my real ear's fuckin burnin a little.

Howie looks in and he says Ew.

I says to him Don't worry, I'm gonna shoo it.

Howie says Throw it out the window hole.

I says to Howie Throw it out the window? The fuck's the matter with you? It ain't done nothin to ya.

Howie says to me It's eating your ear!

I says That ain't *me* in there!

Howie says The rat doesn't know that!

So I point at him and I says If anybody oughta go out the window, it's who's in charge of keepin up the livin conditions here.

He says Oh, you mean the Sing Sing hospitality manager?

I hold my hand out and I says to him You're tellin me you stuff all these fellas in here and you ain't got nobody makin sure is it a place what's safe to stuff fellas?

Howie puts the key in my hand and he says Maybe you haven't noticed, but nobody comes to clean out the cells. This isn't that kind of prison. I don't even think that kind of prison *exists*.

Someone in a cell a few down whispers Is that D'Amato there?

I says to him You're havin a bad dream. Go the fuck to sleep.

The someone what sounds like my pal Hestnaes (hell of a name, right?) says Hiya D'Amato!

I says back to him Heya pal! Then I put the key in the lock of my cell door and turn it.

Or I oughta say, I *try* to turn it.

Howie says to me Come on. Open it.

So I says It ain't openin.

On the ground floor of the block, a door slams. Now we got two voices floatin up to us, talkin about the guy outside what got attacked by a bear. One of em figured maybe the guy died and he was already a ghost, and now he's hauntin the woods. The other one's sayin he ain't even so sure they got bears in this part of the country. Great minds, I wanna tell em.

Howie says The guards are back.

I says I fuckin hear they are. It's only one ear's got the rat on it. Then I try fiddlin the key in the lock. Still ain't budgin.

So Howie hisses at me *Open it!*

I step back and throw my hands up and I say You give it a go, you're such a fuckin locksmith.

Howie steps up and tries to turn the key. Don't turn for him neither.

From the angle I'm at though, I'm seein the flat head what you grab the key by, seein it catch the light's startin to come up through my window right when's Howie rearrangin his fingers like he figures *that's* what's the matter, is how is he puttin his fingers.

I put a hand on his shoulder and I says to him Howie. He reminds me *Howard!*

I says Look. Then I point at the key.

Howie looks. He opens his mouth like he's gonna ask me what am I lookin at, then he sees it.

So he pulls the key outta the lock and brings it up closer to his face. So's he can be totally sure the key he's got's got a big B on it.

I says to Howie When you flashed your pal some cash and said to him Lemme get the key to C Ward, you happen to have a pound of fuckin mattress stuffin in your mouth? Or maybe he's got it in his ear?

Howie's expression gets some kinda fuckin dark, lookin at the key like he's thinkin bout places he can put it might do more good than the lock on my fuckin cell door.

I ask him Why the fuck didn't you peek at the key what's the guy handin to ya, check does he figure the song goes ACBEDFG?

Howie shakes his head and says It's an honest mistake. No way would Franklin fuck me over on this.

I says Franklin's the guy what fucked ya over on this? Where's this Franklin guy at?

Howie says again about It was an honest mistake.

I cross my arms and take another peek at plaster-me sleepin peaceful and easy, cept for the rat on my head. I get to wonderin maybe is it *me* havin the bad dream, am I layin in that cot makin up some kinda yarn's got me standin right outside my prison cell, *wantin* to get in, and not bein fuckin *able* to. On accounta this is a fuckin nightmare.

Then the rat bites on somethin speaks to the structural fuckin integrity of my head. Plaster-me's head caves in, suckin the rat into the skull. It starts squeakin and freakin, scramblin so hard to get out it tips the damn head outta the bed. My fuckin plasterpiece hits the floor and pops like a tomato's been on the vine too long. Like Tomato D'Amato. Ha! Tomato D'Amato!

I have a little laugh to myself about Tomato D'Amato, then I make a pissed face and turn back to Howie and I ask him again, I ask him Where's this Franklin guy at?

Howie says to me Back where we came from. But... Then he looks over the railin to the main bit of the ward, where those two guards're startin up rounds, peekin in to cells. Doin prison attendance.

Which is, this was the fuckin time I needed to be back in my fuckin cell for. Which means I got, what, four minutes to get back in my cell? Assumin they keep walkin slow as they are?

I see one of the two guys is Skip. Course it is. Good ol Skip. The guy what does the left-to-right outside my cell. I always wondered, does he keep daytime hours, tell me Mornin in the mornin and Evenin in the evenin, or is he a graveyard shift guy, tells me Evenin when's he got a pot of joe brewin, and Mornin when's he dreamin of his fuckin pj's? Long shift, either case.

I figure I could blow his fuckin mind by leanin over the railin and askin him. I don't figure I gotta explain to you how come I ain't gonna do that.

Howie leans back from lookin over the railin and slaps his hand over his face and he says Whatever diversion your

I whispers to myself *Diversion.*

Howie don't even stop, he keeps goin with Bear attack buddy got us is over. No way we can get back to Franklin, get the right key, and make it back up here without being spotted.

I look at that second set of stairs they got at the far end of the fuckin catwalk up here, and I think a thought what makes me say to Howie What if we got ourselves a new bear attack buddy? He just blinks at me, so I explain to him I'm tryin to say a *diversion.* What if we got a new diversion?

He asks me Where are we going to get that?

So I snatch the key outta his hand and show it to him, and I says to him B Ward.

MISE EN PLACE:
FRANKLIN

THE WHOLE BRANZINO

FRANKLIN SHRAMM was a man without morals. Fully unburdened by empathy or conscience, there was no depth to which he would not stoop, no outrage against his fellow man he would shrink from committing, to satisfy all those dark little appetites he kept alive on mere scraps of imagination.

However. Franklin Shramm was *also* a man who was tremendously worried about what other people thought of him; specifically, he *really* didn't like it when they yelled at him or were just a little bit upset at him. He didn't think it was very fair, when people were upset with him for the things he did. As a result, though Franklin was more than capable of unleashing unthinkable horrors upon the world, would not have lost a single wink of sleep over committing any number of murders and tortures and whatnot, he never actually did any of that stuff. Because then people would yell at him or get upset with him for unleashing his horrors. And he didn't think that was very fair at all.

Quick, recent example: he cheated on his wife almost constantly, and felt pretty darn good about it. Until one night a few months back, when he accidentally addressed his wife Annie as *Tammy,* i.e. the name of mistress number...oh, who could keep track. Well, he'd done his best to laugh that off, but Annie had just looked at him like, *hmmm.* And Franklin didn't think that was very fair. But he did stop cheating on her after that, just to save himself any future *hmmms.*

His curious moral calculus still left plenty of room for little infractions, though. Little, highly-thinkable horrors that nobody would ever have to find out about. And, consequently, that no one would ever yell at him about.

Like, for example, accepting the bribes that were regularly extended to him by the inmates in his prison.

Well, Sing Sing wasn't *his* prison. Obviously. It was just the one he worked at. Precisely what his job was had never been made entirely clear to Franklin – he'd been hired as a kind of janitor, but had never been provided with cleaning equipment or even instructions. Instead he was a prison guard in everything but title. Franklin assumed this was done deliberately, as janitors surely made less than proper guards. But the point was, Franklin had no clearly stated professional responsibilities, quite a lot of free time, and keys to just about every lock on the grounds.

He was quite popular with the inmates, needless to say, in as much as utility can be leveraged into affection.

THE WHOLE BRANZINO

At least once every day or two, someone on the wrong side of the bars tried to buy his favor. These were always modest proposals: *I know a guy on the outside, he can get you tickets to any show on Broadway you wanna see. Just cadge me a cannoli from Mike's down in Brooklyn, and they're yours.* The goods being exchanged weren't the point, Franklin knew that. What these men wanted was a toe in the door, *juuuust* enough space to wedge their fingers in and start prying it wider, wide enough for them to slip through.

In theory, Franklin would have loved nothing more than to help these guys escape. They could no doubt reward him with significantly greater treasures from outside prison than within. But...these guys were killers. Worse than that, from Franklin's perspective, was that they were all fairly *high-profile* killers. If he helped any of them escape, they would be all over the papers. Even if Franklin's role in the coop-flying was never discovered, he would undoubtedly hear about any unethical hijinks the ex-jailbirds got up to, hear the newsboys screaming about it on the streetcorners. That would be sort of like people yelling at him, indirectly. Which wasn't very fair.

So helping them escape wasn't just a no-brainer, then, but a non-starter.

But hey. He could get the man a cannoli without anybody else finding out, and so take Annie to see *Messin' Around* (which was maybe not the best choice, given that the *Tammy* debacle was still fresh in her mind) at the Hudson. He could slip a prisoner a nudie mag, in return for a solo weekend in a suite at the Ansonia (female companionship was proffered, but Franklin demurred).

All he had to do was hold fast to his principles, such as they were, when someone tried to coax him across his line.

Then Howard had asked him for the key.

Ordinarily parting with a key would be *miles* past the line – too much risk of it coming back to bite him – but this was a fellow employee asking. Howard was also, he'd sworn on an improbable number of loved ones, using it to help a prisoner break back *in* to his cell. More persuasively, he showed Franklin a handful of cash and insisted it was his for the taking, if only he could part with the key to C Ward for just a few minutes.

Franklin had accepted, more quickly than he'd have liked. He would come to regret that haste – the same haste with which he removed the desired key from the ring – several times over. Right about the time the sirens started wailing again, to be specific.

aaaaaaaaWOOOOOOOOOOOGAH. The sound of the siren. The sound of consequence, tapping him on the shoulder and then crossing its arms and looking at him like, *hmmm.*

When he first saw people running, not towards the front of the prison where that weirdo woodsman had shown up and occasioned the first claxon, but *deeper in,* towards the hall from which the cell blocks stretched, Franklin was able to convince himself that the panic had nothing to do with his giving Howard the key to C Ward.

Until he looked down at his keyring, and noticed that the key to C Ward was still there.

What was missing was the B Ward key.

THE WHOLE BRANZINO

Franklin sprang from his seat and rushed into the hall. "What's going on?" he demanded of the blurred figures rushing past. "What's happening?"

aaaaaaaaWOOOOOOOOOOGAH. The siren in the guard tower howled.

"What's happening?!"

A young guard Franklin thought might have been named Pat or something slowed down just enough to shout "riot in B Ward!"

Franklin felt his jaw flop open. "Riot?"

"In B Ward!" shouted another rusher-by.

In that moment, Franklin wanted nothing more than to run screaming from the building, and then the state, and then the country. But he couldn't outrun disapproval. He knew that from experience.

Besides, he had something going for him: friends in B Ward. Prisoner friends, for whom he'd done favors. Cigarettes and books, small amenities that might nonetheless be capitalized upon. Perhaps those prisoner friends might be induced to do *him* a favor now. They'd surely ask for a few things across Franklin's line in return, but there was no helping that. The system had broken down; this was about self-preservation now.

Franklin needed to get that key back from Howard. No matter what. If he could only get it back on his ring, he could deny deny deny that he'd had *anything* to do with *any* unruliness in *any* ward.

Without it, though, he was at the mercy of whomever possessed it.

Didn't take a genius to work out the consequences of

that one. *Hmmm.*

Find the key, he imagined ordering his prisoner friends. *Get it back. By any means necessary.* There was little he could imagine himself unwilling to do in return.

Franklin stopped off at the equipment locker to grab a billy club (self-preservation came in all shapes and sizes), and headed towards the riot.

STEP FOUR:
BAKE TO PERFECTION

THE WHOLE BRANZINO

1

YEAH, I get it maybe ain't ideal I'm openin the doors for a buncha the tri-state's rottenmost fuckin apples, but whaddyagonnado, we needed a fuckin bear attack buddy.

Howie's still fuckin lecturin me about I shouldn'ta given the key to a prisoner just on accounta I figured he looked trustworthy. So I says to Howie I don't see what're you frettin for here. What's the worst what can he do? We *want* he lets out all the bad boys.

Howie shakes his head so hard he kinda loses his balance, on accounta we're walkin real fast to the last place where'd he see Franklin. So he's gotta get himself steady again, then he says to me *Trustworthy,* that's an insane thing to say. The guy you gave the key could be a fucking pedophile!

I says to him Woah, easy there! Just as fuckin likely he

could be a swell fella what returns his library books before when does the stamp say he oughta! You don't know!

Howie says He was sentenced to a *maximum security prison!*

I says Well so was I, you figure I'm a bad guy?

He says to me Yes!

I says Just on accounta I did crimes and murders don't make me a bad guy. You got a prejudice, Howie.

He says *Howard.* And that's not the point. I promised Franklin I'd bring the key back to him, *that's* the point. How the fuck are we gonna get him to give us *another* key when you gave the last one to a goddamned criminal?!

So as we're goin into the stairs I says Watch your head goin through this door, on accounta that's a high fuckin horse you got there.

He turns around to answer me, so he don't see the door on the landin what we're about to reach open up, and he don't see the two guys what got clean uniforms and shiny belt buckles roll out the door.

The guards're both holdin clubs. They're pantin.

Next to me, Howie's shakin fit to mix a drink.

The guards look at me real hard, on accounta I'm the fuckin Platonic ideal of a guy what goes to Sing Sing and riots. And that's before you count I even got my fuckin prison pajamas on still, with the stripes.

Only they ain't comin at me. Gotta figure they wasn't braced for they're meetin a con prior to they hit the ward where's the riot at. Gotta figure doublewise they're confused for Howie's just standin next to me, instead of jumpin on my back and yellin about I got him!

THE WHOLE BRANZINO

So I stop walkin and I says to these guys The fuck are you two outta breath over?

Now they got a split second to decide who the fuck am I. Am I a prisoner what broke outta B Ward? Do I work here and they just ain't seen me before? Am I a fuckin supervisor makin poor choices outta the armoire what picked the wrong time to visit?

I see one of the guys shoot a quick look at the other. Then that one turns back to me and says We heard there was a riot in B Ward.

I says to em This look like fuckin B Ward to you?

Howie's hissin like a fuckin kettle. Full beverage service, with this guy.

The second guard says Uh…no?

I says to him Then what the fuck're you doin here, breathin at me? Get to the fuckin riot already!

Get this: they say to me *Yes sir.*

Yes sir! How do ya like that?

Once the guards are gone, Howie basically shits himself. Well, I don't know did he make the deposit, so to speak, but I figure there was a run on the bank. That metaphor probably don't work, but the fuck do I know about financials, huh?

I says to Howie You wanna keep walkin or what?

Howie says to me Jesus. Jesus. Give me a minute.

I says to him Ain't you never heard the phrase about soonest started soonest done?

He just says This is a mess. This is a goddamned mess.

I give him a little flick on the neck and I tell him Snap out of it.

At least he's outta his fuckin upright coma now. He glares at me and he says Don't flick me!

So I says I ain't gonna flick if we're fuckin movin! Then I flick him again on accounta we ain't fuckin movin.

He says Stop!

I says to him Go! And I flick him again.

Now he's movin. He's mumblin too, but I don't tell him he's gotta speak up, on accounta I figure he ain't sayin nothin's gonna warm my heart.

2

FRANKLIN AIN'T where'd Howie figure he oughta be, and there ain't nobody around who can we ask where'd he go.

Don't neither of us say nothin just then, on accounta we figure we know where'd he go. Same place everybody else seems like they're goin. Fuckin B Ward.

So we're hustlin our way back to B Ward. Lot easier on accounta ain't nobody lookin askance at a big fella runnin *toward* the riot. Most of the folks work at Sing Sing ain't half the size of their fuckin customers, so only thought they're gonna have lookin at me, runnin around with another guy works here, is Thank fuck that one's on *our* side.

While we're runnin, we're layin out a plan in fuckin barebones. Howie's gonna find Franklin. He's small, so he ain't gonna attract nearly as much attention. My job's

I gotta find the big fuck who'd I give the B Ward key to, and I gotta get that key back from him. And I don't wanna say as much to Howie, but now I'm worryin, what if he's got a point there? What if that guy who'd I give the key to *is* a real bad guy? Like a fuckin sex ghoul? Didn't seem like the type, only I gotta figure more fellas're the type than what do I figure. Just on accounta he wasn't lickin his lips and whisperin the word Children don't mean he ain't done an unspeakable pants-off crime.

And puttin to the wayby I maybe figured a sex ghoul for trustworthy, he was a big fuckin guy. So I was figurin it's gonna take some work, gettin back the key.

What I ain't figured was how much of a fuckin madhouse was B Ward gonna be.

We hear it prior to we see it. Sounds like a bunch of fuckin bowlin balls rollin down alleys ain't got no end. Oh, and there's a bunch of people screamin about How come these alleys ain't got no ends. That's kinda what does it sound like.

Then we round the corner in time for seein a guy fall from high up, in a way makes it look like he had some help over the railin.

B Ward's a fuckin madhouse alright. It's like C Ward, a long fuckin five-story rectangle's open in the middle. So we can see on every fuckin floor, you got cell doors standin open, big guys fightin little guys, inmates fightin other inmates, guys with clubs and

BANG! A fuckin gun goes off. Easy to spot where – fourth floor, few dozen yards down – on accounta one inmate goes down, then a guard with a gun in his hand goes flyin off the railin. He hits the ground, his gun goes off again. Hits another guard in the shoulder, who don't take it with grace.

Howie says to me The fuck did you do, Samuzzo?

I says to him I opened a few doors, then I gave the key to some other guy. You wanna chew somebody out, I'll see if I can't persuade that other guy he oughta bring you the fuckin key himself.

Howie just shakes his head and says No. No thanks.

I swear to ya, I can hear his fuckin teeth chatterin from here. I step aside on accounta two guys wanna take their pointy-toothbrush fight through the place what I'm standin in, then I says to Howie What, you scared to go find your guy? Frankie?

Howie says *Franklin*. I'm not *scared*, I just…this isn't my wheelhouse.

I says Ain't your wheelhouse? It's your place of fuckin employ!

He says I don't do riots. I've never done a riot before.

So I says You ain't gotta *do* the riot. You just gotta go *through* it. Look for the other little guy looks outta his fuckin league.

Then I flick him on the neck and head for the stairs, on accounta I spotted the guy who'd I give the key to up on the second floor.

3

I'**M JUST ABOUT UP** the stairs when I'm back at the bottom, and the wrong side up too. My head hits the fuckin concrete, then my neck folds as my fuckin body pinwheels around and slams down.

Takes me a fuckin second to cobble together the what-happened: I suspect the fuckin boot what kissed my nose mighta had somethin to do with it.

I stumble back to my fuckin feet and look up at the stairs. I put my dukes up and square off with fuckin nobody. Ain't nobody comin down the stairs to have a fight with me. Ain't no forgotten enemy steppin outta my fuckin past to settle an old score. Ain't even nobody up on the second floor lookin at me, all proud of he kicked me in the face.

Somebody just saw a big guy comin up the stairs and figured they'd kick him in the face. For the fuckin thrill of it.

I mean look, I get this is a fuckin riot, but that ain't call to be a fuckin jerk. This is how come I tried to start my own Paci-FIST meetins in all the prisons I been to. Bein locked up with other like-minded fellas plays havoc with your fuckin perspective. You got no fuckin vocabulary for resolvin the conflicts. I ain't sayin I'm perfect, on accounta if I happen to figure out who kicked me down the stairs I'm gonna rip off his arms and legs and drop him down a fuckin laundry chute. But once upon a time, and I ain't talkin too long ago, I'd have been so fuckin cheesed about I got kicked down the stairs, I'd probably forget about the key what do I gotta get from the guy and just start unscrewin the feet of everybody's got a little blood on their boots.

Now though, I got me a fuckin vocabulary. So I can take a deep breath and I say to myself, that fella what kicked you in the face, he's doin a fuckin sublimation. He's got somethin in his life ain't goin right, which if I think on it is probably bein in prison, and it's ranklin him so bad he can't figure what could be makin a feelin what rankles that fuckin much, so he figures maybe it's what's right in front of him in the moment what's ranklin. That poor fella's just beside himself in fuckin discomfiture, so best revenge I got is let him fuckin stew. Otherwise he's got *me* doin a fuckin sublimation.

That said, I find the fuck what kicked me, I *am* gonna rip off his arms and legs and drop him down a fuckin laundry chute. But I'm gonna do it for the right reasons, ya know?

Somebody bumps me from behind. Well, some-bodies: three guards swarmin over an inmate like them chompy-ants what you find in the jungle. The inmate's fightin all three of them guards at once, but he ain't so preoccupied he can't say to me Sorry about that.

I says to him You want a hand, pal?

He says to me Nah, I got this, thanks. As he grabs two of the guards' heads and *clonks* em together.

I says to him Course.

Only havin learned my lesson bout anybody could be

a sex ghoul, I says Hey, lemme ask you somethin, what are you in for?

The guy gets a grip on the guard he ain't *clonked*, hand on the neck, and starts shakin him around like a thermometer he's all done with. Then he says, the inmate says to me, he says I got caught.

I ask him I'm askin what ya did. Was it a pants-off crime?

He tries to slam the guard he's got by the neck against the wall, but the other two guards grab onto the inmate's arm so now they're all headin towards the ground. The inmate asks me What?

I explain to him down there, I explain You got your pants-on crimes, standard tough stuff, and your pants-off crimes what ain't fit to mention in civilized company.

He kicks one of the guards on the face – and even from his back, he's got some power there – and says to me Eeeeh...pants-off, I guess. Er. I kept *mine* on, anyway.

I says him Huh. Then I bring the heel of my fuckin boot down on his nose. Then he's just layin there.

I guess you really *can't* tell to look at em, huh?

The guards are rearin around to face me, only I help up the one got grabbed by the neck and I says to em Real sorry I offered a fuckin pervert help. Didn't figure to ask the pants question til after I tendered the fuckin offer. Hopin we're even now, seein how I saved your fuckin lives.

Once I finish helpin up the guard what got his neck snatched, I recognize him. He's from C Ward.

It's fuckin Skip. As in, Evenin Skip. As in, Mornin Skip.

I don't clock the other two guards, so I figure Skip screwed up his fuckin heroics to come help with the riot here, whereas them other two just work here.

In B Ward.

Where I ain't supposed to fuckin be.

We just look at each other's fuckin eyeballs for some number of fuckin seconds.

Then Skip nods at me, real slow. And he says Mornin, Stranger.

I nod back. I say to him Mornin, Stranger.

Then Skip turns and leads them other two off to find somebody else wants to kick the shit out of em. Me, I take the fuckin stairs again, twice as careful. Thinkin bout what if I went and just asked Skip could I use *his* key for C Ward. Figurin just how would that go for me.

4

'LL TELL YA, I'm workin my way over to the guy who'd I give the key to, who's up on the *third* fuckin goddamn floor now, anyway, I'm workin my way over and now *up* to him, and it's like some kinda fuckin showcase for guys got fuckin complexes.

Ain't like nobody asked me, but I figure complexes oughta be called simples, on accounta you ain't gotta take more'n a sentence or two prior to you've got somebody bang to fuckin rights, personality-wise.

Like this guy. He's a big inmate, almost me-sized. He sees me comin and he marks me from twenty fuckin paces. I spot it in his fuckin eyes. He figures me for a notch on his fuckin belt, or maybe on accounta he recognizes me and knows I got a fuckin reputation for a guy ain't a notch on a belt, or maybe just on accounta I'm the only bruiser in the room what can give him a run for his money far as fuckin density goes.

Now we're talkin me from the once-upon, my approach mighta been go high and fast. He's gonna figure I'll come at him guarded so's I can protect my fuckin guttyworks. Only I got strong fuckin, whaddyacallit, *cores*. I got the strong cores. I know from fuckin experience I can tighten up my fuckin tummy and take a blow or two. So I'd do that, if I was fightin like I mighta done, then swing right for the head while's this guy tryna punch out my cores. Then he'd be doublin over, I'd get both hands round the back of his melon and help him out, only I'd lift up my knee for him to rest his weary fuckin head upon, at speed. Then maybe I'da thrown him off the balcony, on accounta you're fightin somebody next to a railin, it's just good fuckin practice to throw em over after ya win.

Only now I got the vocabularies. So I see him comin at me, fists balled up, and instead of fightin I just says to him You look like you got fuckin deep-down aggressions ain't related to your present fuckin predicament.

He don't agree, or else he figures the source of his aggressions is my fuckin liver.

So I tighten up my cores and swing right for the head.

He's doublin over, so I get both hands round the back of his melon and then things don't go how'd I plan on accounta he rolls and hits the ground, then launches right back up and plows into my legs.

Ain't neither of us thought this shit through, on accounta now he's layin face-down on the ground, and I'm layin face-down on toppa *him*, smellin the backs of his fuckin knees.

He does a push up under me. Prior to he can roll out, I scissor my boots together with his head in between em.

He flops back down to the ground.

I scissor the boots twice more, bonk bonk, then I get up and I see there's two other inmates just pointin and laughin at me.

So I throw the first guy over the railin (ya just *gotta),* then I fuckin sublimate at the other two on accounta what, I ain't allowed to have my own fuckin complex?

5

FINALLY CATCH UP to the guy who'd I give the key to right as he's tossin a guy over the railin. See what I'm sayin bout how you got a railin, you gotta toss a guy off it?

Key Guy sees me comin and he says Hey! Look who it is! How's the riot treating ya?

I size him up. He's bigger than how'd I remember him, size-wise. Ain't like I'm worried bout can I take him down...but I figure the play's to come in civil, since that's how's he playin it, then do the first fuckin strike on him.

So says to him I got a complex.

He says I don't know what that means, but okay! Anyway! You like what I've done with the place? Then he lifts his arms up like he's sayin to me Take a look.

I wave my hand round in the so-so gesture. You know the so-so gesture. It's that thing you do with your hand sounds like Eeeeh even if you ain't sayin Eeeeeh. Only I *am* sayin Eeeeh so's I can give Key Guy the full fuckin impact of my sayin so-so.

He says to me What is that?

I says to him It means so-so.

He says I know what it means, but isn't this what you gave me the key for? To start a riot? That's what you said.

I says to him Yeah. Only I guess I'm regrettin it on accounta I didn't figure it'd be so fuckin violent.

He asks me What…did you think it would be peaceful? We'd all just do a sit-in?

I says to him I figure I was bankin on a bit less disassembly, bones-wise.

Key Guy just sort of looks at me and says Okay.

I see him start squarin up. Then I look over the edge of the railin. Three stories down. I ain't feelin so sunny bout its three stories down, seein as I already done two fuckin defenestrations from floor three tonight. Goin over a railin ain't the same as out a window, sure, but you ever heard of the rule of three? It's a comedy fact of the fuckin universe says ain't nothin ever happens twice. You step on a rake so's the handle swings up and breaks your nose, that ain't a problem. You do it a second time, you're fucked, on accounta now you're doin a slapstick routine what's gotta get paid off. Could be tomorrow. Could be ten years out. But you better believe you got another rake handle comin your way. Rule of three. It's just fuckin physics. And it's what's makin me worry do I got another ten-yard tumble comin *my* way.

Then I get a fuckin idea. The most unexpected fuckin way to do a first strike on this guy.

I just says to him Hey, you mind if I get that key back from ya?

He says to me Sure! Then he opens his fist on accounta he'd stuck the teeth of the fuckin key through his fingers so's his punch could have some fuckin bite. He looks kinda bashful while does he hand me the key's got fuckin blood on it.

I take it and nod and I says to him Huh.

He asks me Huh?

I says to him I guess I figured I'd have to fight ya for it.

He says For the key?

I says Yeah.

He asks me Why would I want to fight you for it?

So I says I got no idea. Just sorta felt like, you know, it was fightin got me up here. I just sorta figured fightin for bein some kinda fuckin currency in this current fuckin climate B Ward's in.

He says to me Not everything has to be a fight.

I slap myself on the head with the hand ain't got the key in it and I says I know, right? That's what I'm always

THE WHOLE BRANZINO

tryin to tell people, recently!

He says Do you ever tell that to yourself?

I says to him Holy shit, you'da been a swell fuckin Paci-FISTer! What's your name, pal?

He smiles and says Denny.

I says to him How'd you come by your fuckin wisdom, Denny?

He says I was a teacher, in my old life.

I frown and I says to him How old?

He asks How old was I or how old were the kids?

I says Both. Then I ask him You ain't tickled the kids, did ya? To get ya in here?

Denny flinches and he says *God,* no. I, um...I killed a man. Fit of passion.

I says He have it comin?

He goes all glum and he says No.

I says Ah, it happens. I sure can't judge ya for killin folks. People in glass houses, you know?

He says So what did you

I says to him I knew a guy lived in a glass house once, you believe that shit? It was fully made of fuckin glass.

Denny says Oh.

I says I cut the guy's dead stomach open so I could see what'd he have for dinner.

Denny says to me ...what?

I says I cut the guy's dead

He says Why?

I says So I could see what'd he have for dinner. Anyway. Good talkin to ya. Instead of fightin ya, especially. Big guy for a teacher, huh? Jesus.

He says Exercise helps me relieve stress.

I says to him Denny, you're a good guy, but I gotta get the fuck outta here.

So I take the key and I get the fuck outta there.

6

GET BACK DOWN and I find Howie and I says to him You know, I got some fuckin regrets about how'd I play this.

He says to me Samuzzo.

I says to him Yeah. You put that fuckin bug in my bustle bout every fuckin criminal's pullin double-duty as a goddamned villain. But some of em are nice fuckin fellas, like me.

He says to me my name a second time.

So I says What.

He says to me We have a problem.

I ask him Whaddyamean we got a problem? Only I don't get no further than *we*, on accounta somethin hits the side of my head and I go down.

Takes me a few seconds of rollin on the floor prior to my sight comes back. It ain't been a good day to be my fuckin coconut, lemme tell ya. So it takes a few seconds of I'm rollin on the floor, prior to I can see again. Head's been takin some fuckin punishment today, I gotta say. I say that already? Fuck me, I got an upset tummy all of a sudden.

I start climbin back to my feet when I feel somebody's

got strong hands leanin on my shoulders. So I'm stuck on my knees, some kinda fuckin woozy.

Howie's yellin at somebody Just talk to him! He'll give it to you! He's a reasonable guy!

Another big guy beside me, who I don't figure's the one's leanin on my shoulders, he says to Howie I just watched him throw a guy off the balcony!

Howie says Well he comes on strong, but he's nice once you get to know him!

Another big guy comes over and winds up to clock me in the head.

I says to him You mind goin for the guts? My head's been gettin the fuckin business today.

The guy hesitates for a second, which is when I make my fuckin move. Or I woulda if I ain't just been clobbered in the head. Instead of doin somethin really turns the tables, I just sorta fall forward and land on my face. Lookin on the sunnyside, the guy's fist sails clean over me.

Somebody with big hands, and I don't figure it's any kinda unreasonable if I figure it's the guy what was leanin on my shoulders, matter of fact I'm gonna figure that, so the guy what was leanin on my shoulders grabs me by the fuckin hair and pulls me back to my knees.

Howie says to me They want the key, Samuzzo! Just give them the key!

I says I got the key. I got the fuckin key. Where's the C Ward key?

Big guy to my left, he punches me in the stomach.

I says to him Ylurk. Then I ask him The fuck was that

for?

He says You don't ask the questions!

Howie, he's got some kinda fuckin chutzpah I wouldn'ta fuckin figured him for havin, he punches the guy on the arm and says This is Franklin's fucking fault! He gave me the wrong key! Go tell Franklin to get over here!

The guy Howie just hit says to him Don't hit me.

Howie says to him Go get Franklin!

Guy leanin on my shoulders says Franklin only told us to get the key and bring it to him. He didn't much care to come see how we got it.

I says So Franklin ain't here, huh?

Guy to my right says No.

I says Then who the fuck're ya performin for?

Another tough standin behind me says We're not performing for anyone. We're not *performing*.

I says Then how come you gotta go straight in with sucker punchin me? How come you ain't asked me, like a goddamned regular person, hey, you got the key for us? How come you gotta start right in whalin on me?

Guy leanin on my shoulders says You would never have given us the key.

I says to him Course I woulda. We coulda all gone to see Franklin like a buncha fuckin buddies. Just worked on a guy up there called Denny, he ain't a pervert so I asked him could I get the key back, and that's how'd I just get back the fuckin B Ward key. I used my fuckin words. I got no fuckin use for this key, I just want back in my cell in C Ward.

The bruisers all look at each other. One of em asks me You want to get back *into* your cell?

I says to him Long fuckin story. You guys know what's a whole branzino?

Guy in front of me's eyes dart up to the two guys what're behind me.

Gotta figure those guys behind me're lookin back at him.

Which means I got a second when's *nobody* lookin at me.

I put the B Ward key between my fingers like how'd Denny do, then swing my arm back over my head like if I just threw one of them bowlin balls what were makin such a rollin-thunder racket.

Then my hand's wet, and the shoulder-leaner's screamin. So I definitely hit *somethin.*

I rip my hand hard to the right, then swing up on…*try* to swing up onto my feet, only my feet and the floor ain't findin no common fuckin ground, so I flop onto the shoes of the other guy what was standin behind me and steamroll my whole body up his legs. He flops down onto me just like I done to that one guy up a floor, only I'm fuckin perpendicular to him instead of parallel. So I got a good angle to lift up the key, drive the teeth into his fuckin hamstring and crank crank crank.

I hip-bump him off me, then try to get back onto my feet. Good news is, I get upright with my feet under me. Bad news, I can't keep my fuckin balance, so I start staggerin backwards til I thump into the bars of a cell.

Guy what was on my left is runnin at me now, screamin somethin I figure started as words in his head.

I just open the cell door behind me on accounta it ain't like nobody locked em back up once they got out. Left-side guy barrels right inside. I close the door behind him and lock it again. If I ain't very much mistaken, I hear him say You gotta be fucking kidding me, which makes me laugh.

So I'm laughin when Right-side guy, who I fuckin forgot about, and the two guys behind who I slashed and cranked but ain't killed, all come at me at once.

I lunge to the side, only Left-side's got hold of my fuckin shirt through the bars. That throws me right the fuck off, so I end up teeterin to the side. Lefty loses his grip, and now I'm back on the ground right when do these three fellas *clearly* got complexes get to me and start sharin their fuckin discomfitures.

I roll so's I can get an angle on Right-side's left ankle. I stick the key right in. Slides through smooth enough tells me I probably got it slotted straight between the tendon and the bone. So I crank it to where I figure the teeth are against the tendon, and I start sawin. In out in out in out. Right-side don't appreciate that too much. I got the presence of mind to free the key prior to Righty topples.

I still ain't gettin the world to hold still and lemme back on, so I crawl over toppa Righty and headbutt him once, twice, then he falls asleep. Ain't fuckin ideal, but I'm workin with what I got here. Besides, gravity did mosta the work there.

I roll onto my back and what do I see but Howie tryin

to fight with the two guys what were behind me, so as to keep em fuckin busy. Told ya, guy's got some fuckin chutzpah! I can't believe that shit, ya know?

Seein Howie bein so fuckin heroic juices me. I punch the ground til *it* falls asleep, and I can get back to walkin on it.

Then I get to runnin on it, their precious fuckin key racked tight between my fuckin fingers.

I ain't gonna dwell on it, but let's just say I use the key to lock em down sure as I did Lefty in the goddamned cell, only I done it the sorta way I ain't lookin forward to confessin to Chet about. And if he heard me out and said to me Well heck Samuzzo, now I have to throw you off a balcony, I wouldn't got no choice but to say Fair play to ya. But all the same, sometimes a fella ain't gonna stop comin for ya less ya make so he's *gotta*. Stop, I mean.

Ain't got a fuckin song in my heart about I'm contributin to the fuckin disassembly what's been goin on in B Ward here, but sometimes, what the fuck, ya just gotta stop some fellas, ya know?

After I'm done, I pull some tough or other's tooth outta my fistskin and I says to Howie You happen to catch where the fuck Franklin *is?* Maybe somewhere ain't so full of friends?

Howie just looks at me and points to his chin.

I look at his chin.

He says to me Your chin.

So I feel at my chin, then I pull out the thing's stickin out of it. Can't make it for a second, then I figure it for a fuckin fingernail.

So I reach down and pick up the tooth what'd I pull outta my fistskin and put it in the same hand as I got the fingernail in. I nearly topple fuckin forward, only I catch my balance and find my way back to fuckin standin. Then I smile and I says Maybe I bring these with us, just in case we meet any more fuckin friends wanna know what'd their buddies lend me.

Howie says That's medieval.

I gesture to him we oughta keep movin, and I says Most folks figure me for prehistoric, so I'll take that as a fuckin blandishment.

7

RANKLIN'S COOLIN HIS FUCKIN JETS right outside B Ward. Maybe he didn't have no interest in seein what the fuck he wrought, sendin a buncha goons to have a fuckin failure of communication, but apparently he ain't had no compunctions bout *hearin* it.

We walk out the main door and I go breezin right past the guy, on accounta I figure there ain't no way the weasel boy leanin on the wall right there's gonna be *our* boy.

Then Howie says Ah! Franklin!

So I spin around and I lose my balance and go teeterin, only I get myself teeterin towards Franklin so I shoulder-check him into the wall. I figure if you ain't expectin to see a guy my size comin at you that fast, it mighta looked like that was my what'd-I-plan all along.

THE WHOLE BRANZINO

As opposed to, the big guy lost his fuckin balance.

Gotta figure it worked, on accounta I hear somethin heavy go *clockity-clonk* on the floor. Figure ol Franklin here brought himself a fuckin truncheon what'd I goose him into droppin.

I get the meat of my fuckin forearm under Franklin's neck and press him into the wall and I says to him Since when's it gotta be adults can't fuckin talk on their problems?

Franklin sputters a bit, then after I ease up he says You're a damn lunatic! Opening up B Ward, the hell were you thinking?!

So I says I was thinkin Gee, I need me a fuckin bear attack buddy so's I can find the fuckin keymeister, on accounta he gave up the wrong fuckin key. Then I go back to leanin on him and I says And I was figurin I'd just alert him to his fuckin whoopsie, on accounta ain't nobody ever born got by without a few whoopsies in their whole life. Only I ain't hardly started lookin for him prior to I got four new friends *really* wanna meet me.

Credit where's it due, the guy's meetin my eyes and curlin his lips like he's still got his four buddies flankin him. Flankin Franklin, say that five times fast, right? Anyway, he don't say nothin at any speed.

So I keep talkin and I says Ain't everythin's gotta be a fight, ain't you never heard that before?

Franklin just says to me Where's the key?

I says I don't figure you're seein the point what am I drivin us to.

He says You want the C Ward key.

I says Oh hey, ya do see it!

Now Howie's comin in hot, he says to Franklin I paid you for the C Ward key. You messed up. So make it right.

Judgin from his face, looks like that one got through to ol Frankie boy. I feel him go a bit softer under my arm, then he fishes a great big gypsy-bracelet of fuckin keys outta his pocket. He don't hardly gotta search for the C Ward key, which makes me wonder how the fuck'd he miss it the last time, huh? Anyway, ain't no percentage in leanin on him bout it. He gives Howie the C Ward key, so I ease all the way up and give Franklin back the B Ward key.

As I put it in his hand, he gets a tooth and a fingernail droppin into his palm too.

I says to him Ah heck, forgot those were in there.

He looks up at me and wrinkles his nose. He says Are these from…?

So I says Your buddies. Sorry pal, them's your consequences.

He's back to meetin my fuckin eyes. He looks way deep into em and he says to me But that's not very fair.

So I stick my finger right in his face, then I waggle it up and down and I says to him Fair's for the fairground.

Then I nod at Howie and we go walkin towards C Ward.

Franklin yells at the back of my head Violence is violence!

I turn around to walk backwards so's I can tell him a comeback, and after a bit of stumblin I get on track, only I forgot what was my fuckin comeback gonna be while I was doin that. So I just says to him Hey, fuck you!

I don't figure neither of us'd call that a satisfactory fuckin word-joust.

8

GOOD NEWS IS, ain't no guards hardly anywhere else in the buildin, on accounta there's still a fuckin brawl goin down in B Ward. So gettin up to my cell in C Ward's just a matter of steps and stairs, steps and fuckin stairs.

The other prisoners are up now, but they ain't payin me *too* much nevermind on accounta seein a guy gettin lead back to his cell at weird hours is pretty fuckin unusual, but in a place like Sing Sing…it ain't unheard of, put it that way.

One of the guys yells at me Oy Samuzzo, what's going on out there?

I says to him Riot in B Ward.

Another shouts No way!

I says to him Yes fuckin way.

Third guy yells You look like you were in it!

Another piles on and says Yeah, you look like shit!

I turn to Howie and I says to him I look like shit?

Howie just shrugs and says For a guy who just fought his way out of a prison riot, I think you look pretty good.

I says to him That's settin the bar pretty fuckin low.

He smiles and says Well, I'm trying to set it where you can scale it.

I says I appreciate that.

We get to my cell. I unlock the fuckin thing. Key in the hole. Turn, click. I swing the door open, and I hand the key to Howie, and I step into the fuckin cell. Howie closes the door behind me and locks it. Turn, click.

And that's it. I'm back in.

I'm…in my cell. My little fuckin crimecubby what'd I break outta not half a day ago.

I'm locked the fuck in. Like I never left. If it weren't for the torn-out window bars, and me bein all kindsa roughed up, and Howie standin right outside, I'd be sayin to myself all that shit I just done really *was* some kinda dream. Only there's all that stuff what'd I just mention, so I know I wasn't dreamin.

I slump down on the cot, right on toppa the fake me what ain't got its head no more, and I says to Howie I got all kindsa focused on gettin back in here, I forgot to figure on how was it gonna feel once I got in.

Howie asks me How *does* it feel?

I says to him Not swell, Howie.

He don't correct me on I got his name wrong. I figure he can tell I ain't done it on purpose that time.

I says to him It's just…kinda rotten. On accounta this is it for, what, a fuckin year? I just gotta sit here now. Figure Janis' paperwork does what'd she say it's gonna do, eventually. I gotta figure all my pals're really pals, and they're good like their fuckin word.

Howie says You just have to trust.

I says to him Yeah.

Howie sighs and he says Well… Then he leans his

face between the bars and he says Worst comes to worst, you've got a pal on the inside now. If your friends on the outside don't come through, we can think of

I interrupt him and I says If my pals don't come through, I'm due for fuckin transfer tomorrow. Today!

Howie says Oh. Then he leans back and he says Damn. That stinks.

I says to him I ain't really thought on that too hard. Til just fuckin now.

Howie don't say nothin, which I figure for the right thing to say.

I ask him does he mind givin me some space for I can knock my fuckin thoughts together.

He says he don't.

As he's leavin I says to him Thanks, Howie.

This time he squints at me and he says *Howard*.

I says to him Nah, we're pals now. Pals got nicknames.

He laughs and he says Oh, okay. Sure thing, *Mootzo*.

I laugh too, on accounta now we're even. We both got nicknames don't neither one of us want, but we're still gonna answer to em.

If that ain't what's bein a friend about, I got no clue what is it. Know what I'm sayin?

MISE EN PLACE:
SKIP

THE WHOLE BRANZINO

IT'S A STRANGE SORT OF LET-DOWN, to truly accept death in one moment, only to be denied it in the next.

Not that Skip Tyndale *wanted* to die; he was profoundly grateful he'd survived the riot in B Ward. Really, how annoying would it have been if he'd died there? He didn't even *work* in B Ward. His beat was C Ward, and he was nothing if not a stickler for the rules. It had taken a hell of a lot of yelling to get him to abandon his post, and boy howdy if he didn't regret it almost instantaneously. If he was gonna die *anywhere*, he'd cursed to himself, it...well, it shouldn't be at Sing Sing at all. But if it had to be, C Ward was the place.

Yet B Ward was where he'd made his peace. It was when he and a few of the B Ward guys were trying and failing to take down just one big prisoner, a real tough customer. The guy managed to get Skip by the neck, and that was when it happened. All the classic near-death stuff, the life-flashing-before-the-eyes, the wordless-prayers-to-a-god-he-didn't-know-if-he-believed-in, the regrets-for-risks-not-taken, all that good stuff. He also pissed his pants a little bit, but that wasn't worth dwelling on.

The point was, the sudden and frankly unprecedented-for-Skip reflection upon mortality blew a circuit in his brain. He would have sworn that he'd *heard* the change, a thick, organic *snap*, like something heavy lumbering through undergrowth. It was death, and the moment he encountered it as something beyond abstraction, Skip somehow knew that the only way to confront it would be to embrace it. And so he did.

And then the guy from C Ward showed up.

Skip knew his name – putting aside their twice-daily salutations, anybody who subscribed to a newspaper in the tri-state area knew the name Samuzzo D'Amato – but he still tended to think of D'Amato as *the guy from C Ward*. Indeed, Skip felt fairly confident that if he referred to *the guy from C Ward* in the presence of anybody else who worked at Sing Sing, or even most of the inmates, they'd almost certainly know who Skip meant.

Needless to say, Skip also knew where D'Amato's cell was. Third floor, east-facing wall. In – all together now – C Ward. So what, Skip had wondered, in the kindly fuck was D'Amato doing here in B Ward? He'd wondered it in precisely the way he might wonder if puffins and polar bears lived in the same parts of the world, or how everybody had agreed that six strings was just the right number of strings for a guitar, or any other of those funny little questions that occurred without urgency to a man well into his reefer. Skip hadn't felt particularly invested in what the guy from C Ward was doing in B Ward, because Skip had been about to die. And he had accepted this fact.

Only…he wasn't about to die. And he didn't.

He'd lived, because D'Amato had saved him. Whether or not that had been the guy from C Ward's intention, it was what he'd accomplished. He had intervened, and so saved Skip's life.

Skip was grateful, of course. But to his own astonishment, he was also just a little bit…*disappointed* wasn't the word. As mentioned: he was quite happy to be alive. It was just, well…

It was a bit like studying hard for a test, only to discover that the test had been cancelled. Okay, cool, he'd been spared the most grueling part of the process – but then why had he wasted so much time preparing? In some ways the analogy broke down when one considered the slim interval between Skip's recognition of his incipient demise and his acceptance of the same, but in other ways it held together beautifully – terror dilates time, after all.

There followed for Skip a flow of musings and meditations that could charitably be described as something like pearls, beautiful on their own, but imbued with function and purpose only when strung together.

In point of fact, what Skip cycled through was a fairly pedestrian sort of philosophizing that most people got out of their system without needing to have a brush with death in a prison riot. Some people were late bloomers though, and Skip, like most people who adored rules, was just such a person.

The change wrought in him was not one he could have articulated or anticipated. It made itself known only after the Warden showed up – having apparently not been notified ahead of time that there'd been a rather sizable disruption in his prison – and started trying to piece together what had happened, and how.

It only took a few minutes before one of the other C Ward guards came running into the Warden's office with, as the guard described it: "something, uh, a weird thing." The weird thing was that one of the cells on the third floor appeared to have had its window blown out… or rather, blown *in* from the *outside*, as the bars and debris were now on the floor of the cell. The prisoner was still in the room, sitting on the bed, complaining about having sustained a head injury when the window blew in.

Skip knew precisely who he'd find in that cell.

Sure enough, it was the guy from C Ward, back where he belonged. Samuzzo D'Amato. Skip followed the Warden and the others up to drill the guy, who was, as described, sitting on his bunk, back against the wall, legs splayed, feet flat on the floor.

Samuzzo said to them "A fuckin' owl. You believe that shit?"

The Warden just blinked at him. "What?"

Samuzzo pointed to the window and he said "I'm just sleepin' here, I'm mindin' my own fuckin' business, and an owl crashes into the fuckin' window. Biggest owl I ever seen. Knocks the bars clean outta the fuckin' wall, one of em clonks me on the noggin. That's how come I got the violence all over me, is I got clonked, then I had to roughhouse with this nighttime son of a bitch on accounta I figure he spotted a rat in my cell. We got rats in this place, Warden, you oughta call a guy about that."

The Warden folded his arms and shook his head. "And how big was this owl, then, that you managed to bruise your knuckles against its brittle body?"

"These?" Samuzzo looked at his hands, blackened and bloody, as though surprised to see them. "No, this is from I punch the wall so's I can stay in fightin shape. See?" He pointed to a spot on the wall covered in fresh, red splotches. "I gotta stay in fightin shape on accounta Sing Sing's a real tough place. Word on the grapeline is there was a fuckin riot one Ward over, you hear about that?"

"The word on the grape*vine,*" the Warden purred, "is that you were *there.*"

Skip spoke without thinking: "He couldn't have been, sir."

The Warden looked at Skip the way Samuzzo had looked at his fists. "Hm?"

"Uh…" Skip cleared his throat, and spoke with more confidence. If for no other reason than it was too late to walk that comment back. "I know because he was here when *I* went over to B Ward, and he was here when I got back."

"You just happened to notice the whereabouts of one

prisoner on the third floor?"

"His window had just blown in." Skip couldn't believe the ease with which he was lying to his boss. *Lying* to his *boss!* To be caught now would be to earn himself a cell right alongside D'Amato…but there were more important things than rules. He'd seen that for himself. "I don't know about any owl – he must have chased it off by the time I arrived – but his window made a hell of a racket blowing in."

"Woke me up!" shouted someone from two cells over.

"Made me jump outta my goddamned skin, excuse the language!" Added someone from across the Ward.

The Warden glanced in the general direction that last voice had come from, then turned and fixed his full, corrosive attentions on Skip.

Skip didn't flinch.

The Warden curled his lip, then studied Samuzzo, who'd warped his face into a disturbingly charming smile.

"Oh!" added another of the guards. "There was also that weird guy running around last night."

"Weird guy…" The Warden threw his hands up. "How many things have to go wrong here before somebody calls me?!"

"Uh…I guess more than three."

The Warden considered that for a moment, his head tilting slightly as he processed the conversation to which life had delivered him. "What weird guy was this?"

Skip smiled as the other guard recounted what little

he knew of the man who'd wandered out of the woods, announced he'd been attacked by a bear, then disappeared again without a trace.

"So," The Warden summarized into his palms, "are you...you're implying that this guy blew up D'Amato's window, somehow unlocked all the doors in B Ward, and then vanished?"

"And an owl was there," Samuzzo added.

The Warden lowered his hands from his face, first to glare at his prisoner, then his employees. "Because if that were the case, it would imply to *me* that you're all fucking incompetent. And I ought to fire all of you." He turned to Skip. "Is that what you're implying?"

Skip shrugged. "No more than you staffing a maximum security prison with incompetents would imply your own poor judgment."

The Warden steamed, but did not whistle. He turned on his heel and stormed out of C Ward, fists clenched tightly to his waist.

So...Skip probably wasn't going to be a guard here for much longer. But that was fine by him. Prison is for people who either adore or despise the rules – it's a hard job of work for someone newly positioned in between.

He turned towards Samuzzo. The man on the cot gave him a knowing nod.

Skip smiled and returned it.

Then he went back to his regular beat, for however long it remained his.

STEP FIVE:
SERVE AND ENJOY

THE WHOLE BRANZINO

1

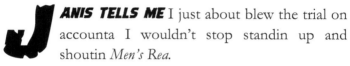 **ANIS TELLS ME** I just about blew the trial on accounta I wouldn't stop standin up and shoutin *Men's Rea.*

First time I said *Men's Rea,* the judge said to me I oughta not do that. Last few times, he starts bangin his gavel and talkin so fast I figure he's tryin to sell me livestock. Janis jumps up on her feet and she's yellin Sir your honor sir! I turn around and Wally's in the back of the courthouse, just shakin his head and smilin at the ceilin.

If you ain't heard, *Men's Rea* is like when a man does crimes what just sorta come out but what he ain't meant to do, like *Dia Rea,* which I figure is how come they sound the same. I asked Janis do they got a *Women's Rea,* and she said to me about keepin my mouth shut and lettin her do her job.

Anyway, Wally's here. Who else we got? Well next to him we got Daff, my girl who's stuck with me well past when she oughta cut and run. Then there's Godric, who I guess figures we're fuckin even for when'd I rough him up on accounta he went and made my life a fuckin labor by loopin in Chet and them other Paci-FIST guys. Speakin of, next we got Chet and Thomas, plus Louie is basically sittin on Chet's lap as per fuckin usual. Gephen ain't showed up, though I heard through the fuckin quote grapevine unquote he made it back to the city alright. He ain't come to collect his five grand what do I owe him, though. Ain't heard from the grapeguy how come, only I got a guess or two. Chet's the grapeguy, by the way, he's been reliable fuckin penpals through this whole last year of Janis is filin paperwork for me.

So and anyway, who else is here? Lotta press guys got little dance cards stuck in their hats. Ain't none of em I got names for, but lemme tell ya, I'm pretty fuckin up on their type, you see what I'm sayin. Fuckin guttersnipes, wha…oh, yeah, Howie's here!

That makes me laugh, on accounta I figure Howie figures it ain't a good look he gets spotted at my hearin. So he came in a fuckin disguise. Terrible one, too. You ever seen them pictures with the Chucky Chaplin guy? Plays a character named The Little Dipshit, got a mustache been trimmed one too many times and a cane so's he can fake disability. Howie's dressed up like that, only he grew himself a full fuckin beard instead of snippin his facials down to how big's a fuckin nickel. I can't hardly look at it without I wanna laugh my cheeks wet.

Does mean somethin to me, he figured he oughta show for my last fuckin court date. Even though Wally already paid him out that money what'd I promise him.

Warms my fuckin heart, I got a courtroom fulla folks got some kinda kindness towards me. Some of em felt so fuckin strong about it they took the stand for me. Howie ain't in that fuckin bucket, only I don't figure I gotta mention how come.

Janis elbows me in the rib.

I says to her Oh hey, how we doin?

The Judge says to me I am going to give you one last opportunity to avoid a contempt charge, Mr. D'Amato.

So I says to him I appreciate that.

Janis hisses *Your honor.*

So I says I appreciate it on accounta my honor. Then I turn to the jury and I says to em *Men's Rea.* Then I give em the biggest fuckin smile I got, and that seems to smooth it all right over on accounta I ain't bein fuckin contempturized.

Ain't too long prior to the judge thwonks his little hammer and says to me I'm free to go. And I gotta figure you might be wonderin, what the fuck happened in the in-betweens there. What'd Janis say, what was her fuckin paperworks, what were the words what a guy wrote a hundred years ago're suddenly good for gettin me outta jail, when I'd figured that for fuckin impossible on accounta there ain't much disagreement on did I do all the stuff they dunned me for usin my fuckin fingertip prints, or else people saw me doin.

Fuck if I know. All the bits Janis ain't needed me to

talk durin, I was just thinkin on how I got a room full of folks what're here for me even though they ain't gotta be, and how that warms my fuckin cockles. Anytime she elbows me, I say what she whispers to me I gotta say, then I tune to a better fuckin station's playin my song.

Then the judge thwonks his little hammer and says to me I'm free to go. He don't sound happy about it, but I figure that's just *His Rea* talkin.

So yeah, what'd Janis say to get me from fuckin point A to point Free, I got no clue. But like that sayin goes, it ain't the journey, it's the fuckin destination.

Yes that *is* how does the fuckin sayin go.

2

COLOR ME FUCKIN STUMPED, whatever color's stumped, probably orange or some shit, color me that on accounta the judge thwonks his gavel and that's all. That's what noise does the law make. *Thwonk thwonk*. That's the difference between I'm spendin the rest of my life in prison, and me bein free as a fuckin bird.

Thwonk.

That's it.

Then ain't nobody's got a problem with I turn around and walk out to where are my pals sittin, only if I'd tried doin this prior to the judge did the *thwonk* a buncha guys might add up to halfa me if they're lucky woulda jumped over furniture so's they could give me a hug from every-which.

Only the judge *did* do the *thwonk*, so here I go, and this time it ain't no bailiffs comin to gimme some fuckin affection.

Oh shit, almost forgot! I turn and I wrap my arms around Janis and she says That's alright Mr. D'Amato, that's al

Then she just goes Ugh okay, on accounta now I'm pickin her up and tellin her thanks for gettin me my freedoms. Since she's askin so fuckin polite, I put her down and head towards the fuckin audience.

Thomas is closest so he tries comin in for some lovin first, but Chet's a fuckin gentleman so he pulls him back prior to I gotta push him. I go to Daff and she's waterin her cheeks so I says to her You better quit waterin your cheeks, or else I'm gonna start waterin *my* cheeks.

She don't quit, so I start. Then we're huggin for a while, til she starts thumpin me on the arm, which is how do I know I started squeezin too hard on accounta I got the runaway affections for her. I'll tell ya, ain't easy lovin somebody breaks like Agnes' tucker, but I figure that's fuckin love, huh?

Then Wally steps on up and I says to him You pulled through for me, Wally. You coulda gone and found yourself another bruiser, but you pulled through.

He says to me There's no replacing you, Samuzzo. Trust me, I've tried!

I laugh and I shake a finger at him like I'm upset even though we both know I ain't and I says to him I fuckin bet you have!

He just pats me on the shoulder and says to me I genuinely have.

I keep on laughin on accounta I know he ain't jokin. But it's a fuckin compliment he says as much to me, on accounta it's provin out I'm just about the only guy alive who's Wally gonna be totally straight with. So I says Alright Wally, what do you got next, jobwise? I wanna get back in the fuckin game!

Janis comes up behind me and says You might want to keep the…*profanity* under control. Because we're still in the *courtroom*. And sound *carries* in here.

I says to her Oh. Sorry. I shoulda said I wanna get back in the *freakin* game.

Daff taps me on the arm and whispers She's not actually talking about the profanity, Sammy.

I give that a fuckin think and then I says Ooooh, okay, I'm with ya now.

Godric gets to me bout the same time as Chet and Thomas, so I point at those second two guys and I says to Godric Appreciate you tryin to help, with trackin these guys down, only it ain't fuckin helped at all. You heard bout the Gephen guy, right? You know he just about fucked the whole thing up, right?

So Godric shakes his head at me and says Calling them was *your* idea. I merely facilitated your

I throw my hands up and I says *Alright,* alright, we're square for what'd I do to your foot. Let it go!

Chet says to me For what it's worth, Samuzzo, I'm really sorry for any disruption caused by our involvement.

I says to him Don't you worry your big fuckin head about it, it all came out like a fuckin photograph.

Godric says to me I knew it would.

I just look at him and I got no choice but I start fuckin laughin. Then I look over his head and I wave Howie over. He does a fuckin hesitation, then turns and books it out the door.

Janis says to me I spoke to him earlier. He'll meet us out front.

So I says Whatsamatter, he ain't lookin to be seen with me?

Thomas chimes right the fuck in and says Given that he was an employee at the prison from which a man escaped, on the same

I says I ain't escaped. Well, I *did,* but

Janis ducks her head and hisses *He's talking about Tear.*

I says Oh.

Thomas clears his throat loud and says *Yes,* on the same night so many other suspicious goings-on occurred, it's probably best he's doesn't attract attention by coming over to congratulate the just-freed criminal.

Janis adds In the *courtroom.*

I says On accounta sound *carries.*

My fuckin counsel, she just nods at me.

So in a big boomin voice I says Well then why don't we let's get the fuck outta the courtroom?

Boy, she wasn't lyin bout the sound carries!

3

IT AIN'T LIKE I BEEN TO SCHOOL when I was a fuckin pup, but I heard about what was it like from kids what did. Well, I heard about what was it like from grown-ups what used to be kids. And it ain't like I'm bringin it up. I ain't callin up my pals and sayin Hey so-and-so, why don't you tell me what was it like when some pinhead told you about how does grammar work? That'd be fuckin peculiar. And I ain't sayin all teachers is pinheads – Denny seemed like a nice fella – just, you know, what gives them the right? Anyway, I was sayin, sometimes you're talkin with your pals, and they mention somethin bout bein young. Bout havin your fuckin child-ass chums, and you're all walkin around in a little gang, and everybody's talkin to everybody else, and sometimes it's ten different fuckin conversations happenin at once, or sometimes everybody's talkin to everybody else bout the same thing. But ain't nobody's gotta feel like they ain't in the little group, even if they're people ain't the sort you'd figure to fit in to the little group.

Like, just as a for instance, if they work at a fuckin maximum security prison what another guy in the group broke outta, then back into.

Or if they ain't got a criminal bone in their body besides bein a fuckin accomplice after the fact, and then just every once in a while durin or maybe even before the fact. That one's Daff, only now that I'm thinkin, maybe it's Janis too. I mean, I didn't never figure I'd have a law-yer what I considered a pal, but some things ain't to be fuckin gainsaid.

So maybe I ain't never had the experience from when was I a kid, but I feel like I got it now. The little fuckin gang of buddies. Daff, Wally, Godric, Chet, Thomas, Janis, Howie. All of us walkin down the sidewalk, chittin and…oh, and Louie, I swear to fuckin Christ I can't hardly tell him from Chet's shadow. Anyway, all of us are walkin down the fuckin sidewalk, chittin and chattin, goin nowhere in particular and ain't thinkin too hard bout it.

Then I stop and I says to em This is fuckin swell, but you know what'd make it even more fuckin swollen?

Ain't hard to tell who knows me the best on accounta they all say it at the same fuckin time. They says A whole branzino?

The ones know me best of all, Daff and Wally and Godric, they know to add the Fuckin right where does it count.

I says to em That's just the fuckin thing. Who else is gettin one?

Howie asks Aren't those expensive?

Louie, whaddyaknow he's got the power of fuckin speech, anyway Louie asks What's a whole branzino?

I says to Louie It's a fish, a delicious fuckin fish what's got the bones in.

He wrinkles his nose and he says Can't they take them out?

I says to him Just on accounta you ain't got a spine

don't mean the fish can't have one neither.

Chet laughs in a way like he feels bad for laughin.

Howie asks me again But aren't they expensive?

I says to him I'm buyin. That's how fuckin high I'm flyin right now. I'm flyin so I'm buyin, howya like that shit?

Then I turn to Wally and I says to him You wanna spot me on this and I'll pay ya back?

He pauses for just a second, then he says Sure, Sammy.

I give him a fuckin embracement, which I ain't the kinda guy gives out fuckin embracements in normal-times, but I'm in a huggy fuckin mood I figure.

Then I says to em all Hang on a second.

I have a little think.

Then I says to em Tell ya what, how about let's why don't you meet me at Rahino's tonight, round eight or somethin. I got one more pal I gotta find.

Howie mumbles about how it better not be Gephen, only he don't say his name on accounta he ain't bothered learnin it, but I know who does he mean.

Janis mumbles about how it better not be Agnes, who's her dotty fuckin ma I one time got halfway friendly with, but *not that half.*

I says to em Ain't neither of those. You gonna fuckin meet me there round eight or what?

They all says they will. So I says to em Sayonara, cept for Godric and Howie. To them I says, I got a question for ya.

Far as they know there ain't no questions where's it

make sense that they're the two guys who would I pick to answer em. Cept they ain't figurin that one of em's real good at findin folks, and the other might maybe be the way to fuckin woo the one I'm lookin to find.

4

YOU GOT TWO KINDS of people in this world: people what ring doorbells and people what knock on the doors. I'm a guy knocks on doors. I don't care how fuckin loud is the bell, a fist's what's really gonna get a fella's attention.

Case in fuckin point, is how this door I'm knockin on opens prior to I hardly put my hand away.

I says to the guy what opened the door Evenin Skip.

Skip gets real scared and tries to close the door, only I put my foot so's he can't. He says I *helped* you! What do you want from me?

Howie pops out from behind me and he says Take it easy, Mr. Tyndale.

Skip relaxes after he sees Howie.

He asks What's going on?

I says to Skip I wanted to repay ya. For helpin me out.

He looks at me sidewise and he says I...appreciate that, but we're even. My helping you out was repaying *you* for saving me.

I says to him that's fuckin swell of ya, only me and my pals are goin to get some whole fuckin branzinos tonight, and I figured you oughta come on accounta we're some kinda pals now.

Now he's lookin at me so sidewise he's just shy of upside-down. He says to me I really…with all due respect, I really appreciate that, but I don't want to get involved with, ah, family business, or

I interrupt him and I says Family business? Who the fuck said anythin bout family business? What family?

He says The

I says What business?

Godric swings out from behind me on the other side and he says to me I think Mr. Tyndale is under the impression that you work for one of the capital-F Families.

So I say Oooooh. Then I says to Skip Listen, I'm a guy works for whoever's got the cash. I ain't in nobody's pantspocket. And you comin to dinner with me ain't gonna put *you* in nobody's pantspocket, least of all mine. I'm just lookin to get some good grub with folks got faces don't make me wanna bop em. You got one of them faces. You want some good grub on me or what?

I figure it's only on accounta I got Howie and Godric with me that Skip says Sure, but at bottom that don't really matter on accounta it's me Skip's smilin at when he says it.

5

SOON AS WE ALL COME IN, Daff and Wally and Janis and Howie and Godric and Skip and Chet and Thomas and LOUIE (look at that, I fuckin remembered!) and me, Raheeq don't seem so happy bout seein us.

He sighs and shakes his head and comes over.

Prior to he gets a word out I says to him You remember me in here bout a year back?

He says to me Of course, yes.

I says to him How I ordered the whole fuckin branzino?

He says to me Two, you order two and then you leave. They go in the trash, *blop*, what a waste.

I says to him You really figure you're more raw bout that than me?

He rolls his eyes.

I says to him Whole year, I been dreamin bout that whole fuckin branzino. Now I brought pals. So we're gonna need...

I look at Wally and he says to Raheeq Ten.

I says Right, ten whole fuckin branzinos.

Raheeq looks round his restaurant what's doin a fair bit of business at present, and he says to me No room, no room.

I take my own look round Raheeq's place and I spot a big ol table's got a whoppin three fuckin people at it. I says to Raheeq Don't you worry bout that, you just get crackin on those whole fuckin branzinos. But not literally like you're crackin the bones. Bones stay *in*.

Raheeq says to me I know about bones. I make the branzino. Do not tell me how to make.

Only he's still finishin up the sentence when I'm noddin at Howie and Chet and Louie, then at the big ol table ain't got but three people at it.

Chet says to me Seriously?

I says You wanna go eat outside on the fuckin sidewalk, be my guest.

Louie, good fuckin shadow he is, he says, and he's givin Chet eyes while's he sayin it like he's wonderin Am I sayin it right boss? Anyway, Louie says to me We can't *threaten* open a table for ourselves.

So I says I ain't sayin we do threats. I'm sayin we loom.

Chet says to me Looming *is* a threat.

I says It ain't a proper threat. It's like you're threatenin a threat you might threaten later, if they ain't receptive to your first fuckin threat.

Chet says Of the threat.

I says to him Bingo.

Daff says to us Hey guys.

We look over and the three people are gettin up from the table, plates in their hands, smiles splittin their fuckin cheeks.

So the rest of us float on over in some kinda fuckin daze, and I ask Daff How the fuck'd you do that?

She says to me I explained that we had a large party, pointed out that smaller table open over there that could accommodate them, and asked them if they might be willing to move.

I says to her Wow! That's my fuckin lady! Then I take another peek at my fuckin party and I realize I was maybe the only one floatin over here in a daze. Ain't nobody else seems half so fuckin flummoxed by what'd Daff do as me.

Raheeq's little nephew kid what might not be his fuckin nephew comes over and asks us quote what would you like unquote.

Godric throws him a bone by gettin his what-does-he-wanna-say out first, he says to the kid Besides the whole branzinos, obviously, is what you mean.

The kid gulps and he says Yes. Besides the branzinos.

I says to him You get us four of the nicest fuckin bottles of grape juice you got, you get my meanin? Then somethin's got tomatoes and bread involved. For a start.

Kid gulps again and he asks You mean, um…the…

I says The illegal grape juice.

He says That's…illegal? We don't have

I interrupt him and I says You're a cute fuckin kid. You go tell Raheeq what am I askin for, then you bring what he gives ya over here and quit your fuckin frettin.

He says Ok…ok. And he goes back to the kitchen.

I call at him And the tomatoes and the bread! I ain't picky on the how do they get along!

Lo and fuckin behold, kid comes back with four bottles of silly grape juice, and we pop em and we're havin a merry fuckin evenin. Me and my nine pals. Some of em I known near as long as my brain's been doin memories, others I ain't hardly known for a year. But you pop a bottle of silly grape juice with somebody, eat tomatoes and bread off the same plate, I figure that accordions them distances in. You're just pals at a table, havin a merry fuckin evenin.

I don't figure I ever had this many pals at once in my

life. Havin em all together at a table, I'll tell ya, it rots me from the inside. In a good way.

We're on to splittin some new sorts of bread and tomato what's got cheese in the equation, when Raheeq comes over. He's got his hands clasped at his tummy, like people do when're they comin to say somethin at me they know I ain't gonna like.

He asks me All is good?

I says You tell me, is all fuckin good?

Raheeq says Ha ha ha, then he says Well, yes, the good news first. The

I interrupt him and I says How bout the bad news first, huh?

He says Yes, well, okay. The bad news is, we search the whole kitchen, up and down. I ask myself, Raheeq, where do you keep fish? And

I just about leap outta my seat and I says to him You ain't got no fuckin branzino?!

He says No no. Then he says Ha ha. Then he says No. Then he says We have the fish. We have, em, here we meet the bad news, we have *nine* of fish.

I says to him We got *ten* of fuckin people.

He says Yes. This is why, this news we meet? It is bad.

I'm some kinda speechless, so it's Wally's gotta ask So what's the good news?

Raheeq says Mhm. The good news is, nine fish? Then he makes a little smoochie noise and he says They will be, *so* so good. I see to this myself.

Then he skips back into the kitchen prior to I got a chance to gather some fuckin words.

So I get up and go after him. Not after him like I'm gonna pop him. Just after him like, you know, I got somethin else to say what I want he hears. Daff puts her hand on my arm to try to stop me, so I explain to her the difference. She don't take her hand off my arm, only she ain't fightin I slide out from under it.

I catch Raheeq and he says to me I am so sorry, I have no options, where do I buy fish at this hour? There are no more fish than nine!

I says to him That ain't a problem. I ain't mad, honest. I'm just tryin to tell ya...you give the whole fuckin branzinos to everybody but me.

Raheeq looks so fuckin confused for a second I figure maybe I was just goin *wahbwahbwahb* instead of sayin what'd I say. Then Raheeq says You will give the fish to others?

I says to him Sure I will.

He says Fish for everyone but you?

I says to him You got it.

He does just one Ha, then a second Ha. Then he says My friend, you are truly a graceful man!

I shrug and I says I'm just tryin to do right by my pals.

Then, almost like it's a by-the-way, I says to Raheeq as I'm headin back to the table, I says How bout you bring me a plate anyway, huh?

6

SEE, I got this all fuckin figured out. I'm doin the nice thing, lettin everybody else have the whole fuckin branzinos. They're all fully fuckin in the know bout how've I been yankerin for this fish for a fuckin year. Then they see I'm givin it up so's they can all have it? My pals here, they're gonna feel so much fuckin fellowship at me, they're gonna all chip in and offer me a ninth of their fish. One ninth. Ain't nothin to them. Nine people at the table got nine fish, everybody offerin me a ninth, boom, we got a tenth whole fuckin branzino for me. And it ain't no small thing, I'm gonna get some fuckin pal points outta this too, how'd I let everybody else have the whole branzinos.

So the fishies show up and the server kid puts an empty plate in fronta me.

Thomas says to him That's cruel.

The kid says Uh?

Thomas tells him Taunting the man by putting an empty plate in front of him.

So the kid grabs the empty plate and says to me I'm so sorry, I thought you asked for it.

I says Ah ah ah. Then I take the plate back and put it down in fronta me, and I says to him Bye kid.

So everybody starts eatin their whole fuckin branzinos. They're all pushin the bones around to get at the meat, noddin their heads and goin Mmm.

THE WHOLE BRANZINO

I'm figurin any second now, somebody's gonna get generous. Ask me do I want a bite, somethin round about maybe a ninth of their fish. I'm figurin Daff'll be first, but maybe Wally'll step up. Or Chet, he seems like a fella's got a big fuckin heart.

Look at em, shovelin it in. Ain't nobody's hardly takin the time to breathe, cept for they can draw enough to go Mmm.

I tap my finger on the table. Just the finger, on accounta I ain't lookin to get a fist's-worth of nevermind. Just the tap tap tap.

Any fuckin second now.

Then my mouth opens up and I says with it, I says Ain't nobody gonna offer me some?

All of em just chew at me.

I point to my plate and I says to em I'm the one wanted the whole fuckin branzino so bad, and I'm sittin here with a plate ain't got nothin on it cept crud from whatever fuckin fettuccini bullshit was on here last.

Skip says I think fettuccini would be served in a bowl, if it had a sauce.

So I says to Skip You shut your fuckin mouth, if I hadn'ta invited you I'd have myself a whole fuckin branzino right now.

Skip shuts his fuckin mouth, only he's got the last fuckin laugh on accounta he's shuttin it full of fuckin fish.

Daff picks up her plate and moves it towards mine and says Here, you want some? You can have some of mine.

I says to her I don't want you givin it to me in that fuckin voice.

She leans back and asks me What voice is that, Sammy?

That gives me a pause, so I wait for somebody else starts talkin.

Chet says to me You wanted us to share our fish with you?

Then I point at him and I says *That's* the voice I ain't likin.

Chet just blinks at me.

I says to him It ain't fuckin brain science, or whatever the fuck's the sayin. You all see how'm I bein so fuckin generous, then you have this real fuckin touchin moment where do you all gimme one ninth of your whole fuckin branzinos. Then I got a whole fuckin branzino of my own, which is some kinda fuckin sweet on accounta the power of bein pals or what the fuck.

Godric says to me But then you would be the *only* person at the table with a whole branzino. We'd all have just eight-ninths of one.

I says to him That ain't my fuckin problem, you got a whole fuckin branzino or not! I done a nice thing for ya!

Janis says to her fish Okay. Then she stands up and she says to me I'm going to go. You can have the rest of mine, Mr. D'Amato.

I says to her I don't want the fuckin rest of yours! I want a ninth! SIDDOWN!

Janis siddowns.

I says to em Ain't none of you fuckin screws ever had

276

pals before? I gotta explain to you how do pals treat each other? You be fuckin kind and shareful and don't be so fuckin selfish, and you see your pal ain't got a fish and he really fuckin wanted one and there's nine of ya, you all give him one fuckin ninth so's he got his WHOLE. FUCKIN. *BRANZINO!*

Now they ain't even chewin at me no more, they're just starin.

And then I see Chet's eyes. He's lookin at me in that way's what I figure how does a sad dad look at a kid what let him down, and for a time ain't even the first time.

I don't give so much of a shit about Chet. It's when do I look over at Daff, when I see how's she lookin at me, that my heart drops to my fuckin feet. Like a fuckin lovewise defenestration from floor three, metaphorwise. Rule of fuckin three. I oughta known it was comin for me.

So I clear my throat and I sit up straight as a fuckin arrow what's still in the long bucket, the...the quiver, and I figure out a voice is gonna sound some kinda truthful and I says to em I'm just yukkin, guys.

I can tell who'd I fool by my sayin I'm just yukkin on accounta they're the first ones to laugh. And its Louie. Louie says Ooooooh first. Then he says Ha ha ha.

I just throw my shoulders up and I says to em all Hey, ya know, you spend a while in a buncha real nasty lock-ups, you get used to tellin jokes got punchlines with brass knuckles. I figure I gotta adjust to bein out with the regulars again, ya know? With my jokes. Seein as I was fuckin jokin. And we all see that, how was I fuckin jokin.

Louie stops laughin on accounta he sees Chet ain't laughin, but then Chet starts laughin so Louie is back at it.

Howie starts forcin a chuckle, pretty obvious about he's forcin it, and he says to em Right…that's just some of that classic Sing Sing humor. I hear the inmates making those jokes all the time. Then he starts warmin to his fuckin lie and he says Yeah, I'm just so used to it I assumed everyone got the joke.

Skip says Right…classic Sing Sing.

Then Wally says He even used to make those kinds of jokes *before* he went to prison.

Godric jumps in with Yeah, that's really the classic Samuzzo sense of humor.

Janis don't say nothin, but for her that's basically the same as agreein.

Daff's still just lookin at me. But it's back to how does she usually look at me. Kinda like she's rememberin a joke she heard a while ago, only she can't recall how does it go, only she remembers how'd it make her feel. Which is a kinda way lifts my heart back up to where's it supposed to be, bein looked at like that. By her, anyway.

Everybody else though, they're fallin all over themselves to vouch for I was kiddin to each other. And I'll tell ya, this ain't the same as I'm gettin myself a whole fuckin branzino, but I gotta figure it's near as ya can get without you got the fish right in fronta ya. On accounta if bein a pal ain't about sharin your fuckin fish, I figure it's got somethin to do with not bein too hard on your pal when they says to ya Gimme some of your fuckin fish. And sometimes its about pretendin you buy he was yukkin about that, even when all of everybody knows that weren't the case.

Don't get me wrong, I'd rather I'm gettin the whole fuckin branzino, just on a plate for me, so friendship ain't gotta enter into it at all. But without I'm gettin that fish on a fuckin plate...well, it's how'd I just fuckin say it is.

DIGESTIF:
SAMUZZO

THE WHOLE BRANZINO

WHEN SAMUZZO FOUND OUT the meeting was on Staten Island, he asked if it could be moved to somewhere else. Anywhere else.

"You know," he told Godric, "thinkin on it, I ain't sure have I ever even made it to Staten Island or not."

Godric adjusted the little visor on his head and said "all you have to do is get on the ferry. The new client will meet you at the dock."

"I'll try, Godric. I swear to ya, I'll try."

This first job post-trial was going to be a small one. At Daphne's suggestion, that was – the trial had been big news, regionally speaking, and it was her belief that more people than ever were going to recognize Samuzzo's face from the papers. His mere presence in public was going to attract unwanted attention. Not that discretion had *ever* been his strong suit, but even still.

That was what Wally had said about it. "Even still." He'd agreed with Daphne about going for a small job, as had Godric.

Fine by Samuzzo, if for no other reason than this new client was one who might have other jobs for him down the line. Bigger ones, to be done after a few other faces had hit the news. The public had such a short memory, after all. That was what Samuzzo said about it. Not as many people agreed with him.

Point was, this wasn't a meeting to miss. Which was why it seemed crazy to hold it on a goddamned island. There were so many nice diners in the city. Which, Manhattan was also an island, but whatever. The client said Staten Island, so down to the docks Samuzzo went.

It was a nervy hour or two, but he eventually got on a ferry, feeling something close to certain it would take him to Staten Island. That done, he settled in to one of the inside seats and looked out the window.

The ship pushed off a few minutes later. It whistled a few times as it bade the city goodbye. Samuzzo jumped at each shrill report.

Somebody sat down next to him. Right next to him. When there were so many other seats open in this car.

Samuzzo turned slowly, frowning down at the little guy sat beside him. A stringy little fella in a maroon suit, this was, head aimed straight ahead, eyes flitting so fast in their sockets Samuzzo would have sworn they made a soft *thwip thwip* noise.

"You're the guy from the papers," the stringy little

fella said.

"You keep talkin to me," Samuzzo replied, "you will be too. Obituaries section."

To his credit, the stringy little fella didn't budge. "You're muscle for hire." Again, not a question.

Samuzzo said nothing. He had thought that line about the Obituaries section was pretty good. Couldn't think of a way to top it.

The stringy little fella glanced over his aisle-facing shoulder, then leaned in towards Samuzzo and said "I have a job for you. I have money."

"I ain't lookin for a job."

"I have money."

"Oh, we playin like there's an echo? I ain't lookin for a job."

Clearly, this stringy little fella had thought his line about having money was pretty good too. He shifted around a bit and said "I sometimes wonder if something couldn't *happen* to my wife."

Samuzzo groaned and stood up. "Those ain't my kinda job, you fuckin flapjack. Assumin I even *do* jobs, which is an *allegedly. Mens Rea,"* he added, as he forced his way back out into the aisle. Making no effort to avoid stepping on the stringy little fella's feet as he went.

Grumbling, aware of strangers watching him as he passed, Samuzzo stepped through the door, and into the next car. He...

...

He paused in the space between the cars. The cars of the ferry. Which were currently rattling along on tracks.

"Fuck me," he announced, as he completed his journey into the next car. He sat in an empty seat, then glanced over to the well-to-do stranger sat across the aisle. "Hey lady," he called to her. "This ain't the Staten Island Ferry, is it?"

She couldn't seem to decide whether to narrow or boggle her eyes at him. So she settled for oscillating between both extremes very quickly. "No. This is a train, sir."

Samuzzo looked out the window behind her. Goddamnit. Should have known something was up when the ferry was traveling on the land, instead of the water.

"Say," the woman said, "aren't you that criminal I read about? Who was recently released from prison?"

"I got no clue what do you read about," Samuzzo replied unhappily, still staring at the landscape streaking by over the stranger's shoulder. "Hey, you know where's this fuckin thing headed?"

"California."

Samuzzo sighed. "You know does it got a stop in Jersey or what?"

"I don't believe so. But..." The woman scooted from the window to the aisle seat, moving nearer Samuzzo. She glanced up and down the aisle, then leaned across it and whispered. "I am a lady of means. And I may have a problem to which your unique skillset may serve as the solution."

"Yeah," Samuzzo sighed again, "who the fuck don't."

The train made a few stops before California, but Samuzzo slept through them all.

Samuzzo D'Amato will return in

PAY UP, GULLIVER!

Made in the USA
Middletown, DE
24 October 2023

41295484R00172